IT'S OKAY
TO BE
BROKEN

Holly L. Wright

NCREATING
SARASOTA

3 1969 02393 6908

I would like to dedicate this book to my children
Savanna, Sydney, and Payton.
Each of you have given me the will to be strong,
keep fighting,
and never give up.
I am so proud to be your mom.

ACKNOWLEDGMENTS

I would like to express my deep appreciation and gratitude to all of the family, friends, and community who provided support and encouragement to our family during the most difficult time of our lives.

I want to thank my parents, brother, sister, and in-laws but especially my mom, Sybil Porter, for her selflessness in helping our family during Payton's illness. Savanna and Sydney are the women they are today because of you.

I want to thank every sponsor and each person who participated in the events that supported us. There are too many of you to name but you know who you are.

I want to thank the amazing Nikki Odimba for believing in me and believing in Payton's story. You saw my vision and were able to express, in beautiful words, that it is "okay to be broken." Our island awaits, my dear friend!!!!

I want to thank my darling husband, Patrick, for being my rock. You are an amazing husband and father. I am so blessed to have you in my life.

"Life is not the way it's supposed to be.
It's the way it is.
The way you cope with it is what
makes the difference."
~Virginia Satir

IT'S OKAY
TO BE
BROKEN

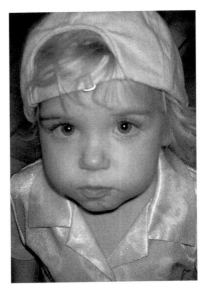

"God, I am begging You. Please, please help my baby girl. She can't suffer like this. She's only 4 years old!" I shouted to Heaven from inside my closet.

"Please God. Help me. Help us. I…can't. You…You have the power to heal her. Just heal her! Please! Please! I beg You! Take me! Take me instead. Give her my health and give me her cancer. Do it!!!"

There, lying on my closet floor with bloodshot eyes from endless tears and hair matted with sweat, I pleaded for help from the only Person that could.

"Don't take my daughter from me. Please God. She can't die."

CHAPTER 1

Happy New Year!!!" we all screamed!
Patrick, my husband, leaned over and kissed
me. We smiled, knowing the upcoming year
would be a great year for us.

We were healthy. My three daughters were growing
up fast. Beautiful home. Wonderful family and friends.
Life, as far as we knew, could get no better.

Snuggling into bed after a long New Year's Day,
I laughed as I remembered some of the resolutions
I'd heard people making. We all knew they would
be forgotten or neglected by February. Still, it was
always fun to make them.

Sleep almost had me under when Payton,
my youngest daughter, made her almost nightly
entrance into our bed. Every night we put Payton
in her bed, which was located on the opposite side

of our home. Nevertheless, each morning, we woke up with her little toes in our ribs or her long hair sprawled across our faces. We didn't mind her sneaking into our bed. I was never a "…the-book-says…" type of mom. Anticipating there would come a day when she would grow up and not want to be in our bed, we held onto this phase of her wanting to snuggle with us.

On this particular night, Payton began to cry and complain that her bottom was hurting. I rubbed her bottom and back and tried to coax her into sleeping. No success. The crying continued. No longer sleepy, I wondered if she'd fallen on her way to our room or if she'd been bitten by a spider while playing outside earlier that day.

I took her to the bathroom and checked her bottom really well. Nothing. I gave her a little Tylenol to alleviate the pain and she fell asleep, for a while. As soon as she woke up, she picked up where she left off the night before. We had no choice but to take her to the emergency room.

"I wonder if something is really wrong," Patrick said, holding Payton. Savanna and Sydney, our first two daughters, always acted like Momma's girls. Payton—definitely a Daddy's girl.

CHAPTER 2

All I've ever wanted to do was have a family, be a great wife, and become a mom. I'm the middle child. I have an older sister and a younger brother. We're all very close. Kym is only 2 years older than me and Brian is 6 years younger. We spent the weekends at my grandparent's house, took family vacations, and spent a lot of time playing board games. Yes, we were *that* family. Therefore, the picture of a great life, in my head, has always placed family first.

My mother can tell you that as a young girl, I talked about finding "the one", getting married, and having babies of my own. Can you tell I'm a planner?

Well, the plan began to unfold just as it should, just as I'd planned. I graduated high school. Check. I began college in Pennsylvania. Check. I met the love of my life, Patrick Todd Wright. Check. I married him at 20 years of age and began to form the foundation for my new family. Check.

Then, my plan began to unravel. I dropped out of school and began to work as an Administrative Assistant making $600 per month! (Obviously, not one of my best decisions.) I hated that job. Nothing against the people who worked there but I KNEW I could do more; I knew I was settling. I'm not the type of person that finds comfort in mediocrity, not if it is within my power to change my circumstances. So, I decided to go back to school.

When I submitted my two weeks' notice to my manger, he said, "I'll just keep the position open for you. You'll be back. You're not the school type." It was just the fire I needed under my behind to make sure I finished.

Working full-time and pursuing my degree was no easy task. Exhausted and overwhelmed are not the adjectives you want in your life, especially at the same time! Thankfully, Patrick was a very supportive husband. He worked long hours to support us. Earning my degree was really hard but I did it, twice. I received my Bachelors & Masters degrees. By the time I finished, I was 26 years old.

CHAPTER 3

Our ER visit was fairly simple. After a very long wait, Payton was examined and we received a diagnosis of growing pains. They released us. As days grew into weeks, Payton continued to complain. The pain had moved to her leg.

We massaged her and gave her long, hot baths but nothing alleviated the nagging discomfort. Soon, she began to limp. Back to the doctor's office we went. They took more X-rays and again, nothing. As a final step, they told us to find an orthopedic doctor and have them examine her. We found an orthopedist. When Payton was checked by him, he said, "This is probably just growing pains. She'll be fine." They then released us.

The crying wouldn't stop. Our lives seemed to turn into bone scans, blood work, more X-rays, and still…nothing. No reasons that answered my "why" questions. Meanwhile, Payton continued to walk with a limp.

We both were lying on our backs one night, staring at nothing, overwhelmed by everything. *Heal my daughter,* we thought at the same time but the room remained silent. Sleep avoided us. After lying in bed for almost an hour in silence, Patrick said, "I'll take the first shift. You try and sleep."

We knew we needed to sleep but the anxiety and stress would keep us up for hours, days, until our bodies collapsed from exhaustion.

"Okay," I said quietly, knowing sleep would never come.

I wish I could remember the many times we called her pediatrician's office, how many visits occurred as we searched for the root of the problem. Finally, we were told we were probably dealing with diskitis or juvenile arthritis. A small sigh of relief escaped us because we *almost* knew what we were dealing with, or so we thought.

CHAPTER 4

From January to April 2006, Payton continued to complain as we searched for answers to her ailment. For her 4th birthday, she wanted a dance party. We gladly obliged, hoping the party would make her happy. She loved the music but she was in so much pain, she couldn't participate. The dance instructor created sitting games for the kids.

Immediately following the dance party, we packed up the car and kids and headed to SeaWorld. It was the first time Payton had traveled such a distance in her car seat since she'd begun to complain of pain.

As Patrick drove, we observed Payton stiffen up and shift in her car seat. Then the tears and shouting started, "My back hurts, Mommy."

"This is ridiculous," Patrick said, frustrated from seeing his daughter suffer. "That's it. When we get back, I'm going to find out when the Rheumatologist is on call and drive her to the ER. Then, he has to see her." My husband took charge.

After months of getting the runaround, Patrick and I finally had a plan. Since there was only one Pediatric Rheumatologist, a new appointment with him would take 3 months. We'd already spent almost 5 months trying to figure out what was wrong with Payton. Sometimes, you just have to be a strong advocate for the people that need you. We were going to just…show up.

During this time, as if we didn't have enough on our plate, I came down with the absolute worst flu I'd ever had in my entire life. If you've never had the flu, thank your lucky stars. For those who have experienced this onslaught, you understand what I went through. I could not get out of bed. Patrick was overwhelmed trying to take care of all of us. We'd told my mother of our plan to take Payton to the ER to see the only rheumatologist in the state and she was so worried, she flew down from Pennsylvania to help us. As always, she wanted to be there for us.

"I'm sorry to leave you when you're sick, babe. Your mom and I are going to take Payton to the ER, because that doctor is on call. We've gotten

Sydney and Savanna ready for school and I've made arrangements for them to have a ride home in case we get delayed at the hospital."

"Patrick, call me AS SOON AS you know something," I groaned. Ironically, I was so sick, I couldn't even get out of bed.

"I will. As soon as I hear, I'll call you."

CHAPTER 5

Dr. Morelli.
It's hard for me to even write his name without tears rushing to my eyes. He is such a remarkable person and doctor. In the ER, he was the first doctor to examine Payton.

Initially, he thought Payton's body might be fighting off an infection. The plan was to keep her overnight and give her antibiotics to fight the infection.

"Hol, they're going to keep her overnight and give her antibiotics. They suspect it's an infection."

"Thank God!" I managed to get out. Finally. After months of not knowing what was happening to Payton, we had answers. But as Patrick recounted more details to Dr. Morelli and told him about all the steps we'd already taken, the things we'd been told, and the inability to get an appointment with the rheumatologist, more of our prayers were answered.

"Oh, that's my former partner. I'm pretty sure I can get him to see your daughter," Dr. Morelli said. Coincidence, I think not.

The next step Dr. Morelli took changed our lives. He completed a simple pressure point test down Payton's spine and she winced immediately.

"Hmmm. Let's get an MRI done on her. Hopefully, this is diskitis."

Normally, it takes a few days to get the results of your scan. This time, less than 30 minutes.

"They found a tumor in her pelvic area, Holly."

"What?" I sprang up from the bed. I was too sick to scream but I remember completely losing it on the phone. Patrick's second call sent me into hysterics. One of my girlfriends had just brought Savanna & Sydney home and they found me, in tears.

I couldn't think. My mind jumped from thought to thought, question to question. A tumor, in my 4-year old? Nothing made sense. Patrick could tell I needed help processing the situation and sent my mother home to be with me. When she arrived, I was slumped in a corner of the room, trying to get as far away as I could from the possibilities.

"Mom, really? A tumor? Is it serious?" I asked, trying not to think the worst.

"We just have to wait and see. It could be," she answered honestly.

CHAPTER 6

Payton's biopsy was scheduled for the next day and I begged the doctors to let me see her, promising to mask up. Naturally, they were concerned about the potential to spread germs.

I remember praying very hard and hoping I would find the strength to make it to see my baby. Before the sun was up, I was dressed. Nothing, not the thumping in my head nor the extreme nausea, could keep me away from my baby girl.

When I walked into her hospital room, her face lit up. My Payton. I didn't want to make her cry or scare her so I simply laid beside her. She rubbed *my* hair. She soothed me.

"Mommy, I feel so bad that you're sick. I hope you feel better," she said, her little eyes concerned about my well-being. That's Payton. The nurturer.

Always putting others before herself.

Our immediate family filled Payton's room. My parents were there as well as my in-laws. Soon, they wheeled her gurney into the hallway and I must admit, the lump in my throat became unbearable. As we all stood around her, waiting, Payton looked directly at Patrick and said, "Don't cry Daddy. It's gonna be a good day." (Do you see the strength in my baby?) Unbelievable.

The entire family moved to the waiting room, because we were told that the doctor would address everyone there once the surgery was over.

"Okay mom. You can't be in the waiting room. Keep your mask on and wait in Payton's room."

CHAPTER 7

Time sure can play tricks on you when you're waiting. Minutes felt like hours and before I could go and demand answers from someone, the door swung open.

Imagine my surprise when the neurosurgeon walked into the room, where I sat alone, and seemingly without any type of concern or empathy, flatly announced that my daughter, MY DAUGHTER, had cancer.

Everything stopped. Time. Breath. My heart. The flu. Due bills. All things petty – stopped. Everything completely stopped except for the mouth of the most unprofessional doctor I'd ever met!

I understand that doctors have to put up an emotional wall in order to keep their own sanity, but the callousness and disrespectful way he treated us was uncalled for, for I believe that compassion is *still* a critical part of dealing with people.

Use your imagination to experience that moment with me: I was extremely sick, so sick that I could barely stand up for more than a few minutes. I was alone. I felt overwhelmed and disrespected. I sat on the hospital bed, drowning. Suffocating. Dr. "No Class" did not pause when he saw the color fade from my face, IF he even saw the color fade from my face. I knew he was talking but he sounded like Charlie Brown's teacher. Meanwhile, my mind was trying to think of one person with cancer in my family. Just one. No one readily came to mind.

My brain simply could not comprehend what he was saying to me. Cancer, in a 4-year old? *This has to be a mistake.* In the midst of the chaos growing inside me, my minister walked in with Patrick not far behind him.

"I thought you were coming to the waiting room…" Patrick started, until he saw my face.

"No, I'm here," Dr. No Class answered smartly, as if we were disturbing him.

"Will you, will you…repeat what you said to me…to my husband?" I whispered weakly.

Sighing as if I'd asked him to do something

unrelated to his job, he replied, "I don't think I need to repeat it again. You can just tell him." Asshole. (Excuse my language.)

If it had not been for Pastor Steve, who kindly but forcefully requested that he repeat himself, he may have simply walked away. You could tell he was absolutely irate about having to explain to my husband that our daughter had cancer. As soon as he possibly could, he left the room.

There we sat. In silence. In shock. *How can this be happening to us? This can't be real. What's going on? How could my world be normal and then…?*

CHAPTER 8

Eventually, they brought Payton back from surgery. Again, I didn't want to scare her. I just wanted to hold her and wake up from the gripping nightmare. I stared at my little one. She looked the same. How could such a ravenous disease be growing inside of her?

"I want to walk," Payton announced. They didn't want her trying to walk around too soon but one hour later, she was sitting in the kid's room, painting. Such a strong little girl! Her strength gave me strength. The fighter stood up inside of me and snapped into action.

"Okay, it's cancer. We're going to fight it with everything we have."

At the time, Patrick was working as an Executive

Recruiter and immediately did what he did best, he started to search for the right people to handle this job. Patrick called all the top hospitals and had Payton's records sent to them because of the case's complexity.

I didn't want to hear any reports or updates because I knew it would sap every bit of strength and hope I had scraped together. I therefore became the caregiver. Payton's care was going to be top notch if I had anything to say about it.

The hospital did not have a Pediatric Neuro-Oncologist. For 3 weeks, we waited for a consensus about what *type* of cancer we would face. Various reports rolled in but each presented different results. However, a reoccurring prognosis was PNET, Primitive Neuroectodermal Tumor. This was a rare, malignant cancer that offered a 70% survival rate... on average. 70%! Not good enough for me. That number was too low for my liking and I could not stop thinking about the 30%, those that didn't make it. No, I wanted a 100% survival rate. Surely with all of the advances we'd made, we could cure this cancer. Right?

Finally, after countless consults, we received the concluding answer. Payton was sent to play with a Child Life Specialist while the doctor spoke to us. I think it was the sigh she released before she started speaking that made my stomach drop. Patrick and I looked at each other, hoping she'd tell us that they were wrong. I wanted her to say, with absolute confidence, that our daughter would be okay.

CHAPTER 9

It's Medulloepithelioma. A very rare form of brain cancer. There have been less than 10 cases in the United States, less than 40 in the entire world. No survivors. At this point, you have hope."

"Hope? What do you mean we have hope?" I asked, puzzled, reeling from the death sentence she'd just delivered.

"ALL," she emphasized, "You have is hope. We can't cure this. We'd give her five weeks."

"To do what?" I asked, obviously in shock.

"Live."

Patrick and I turned to the TV monitor and looked at our rambunctious 4-year old, playing and laughing.

"Wha—" is all that came out as I tried to speak.

All you have is hope. All you have is hope. It kept echoing in my head.

"I'm sorry. We can put together a plan to slow it down but honestly, there is no specific protocol for this type of cancer. The other option is to…" she trailed off.

I can't imagine how I looked, standing there with my mouth open. Body frozen. Almost catatonic. *Was she about to tell me to just…let go, not fight?*

How in the world do you tell someone their 4-year old only has 5 weeks to live? How my body remained upright and functioned is beyond me. God must have given me strength because the *inner me* buckled. I wanted to curl up and hide.

"Doctor, if this was your daughter, what would you do?" I asked.

"Fight. I would fight."

The doctor excused herself and Patrick and I were left alone. *Five weeks left to live.*

"Did she," I started, "Did she just say I'm going to bury my daughter?" I asked aloud. Patrick looked like a ghost. We turned to look at the screen again. Payton was participating in a Bingo game, wearing a pink cowgirl hat and laughing up a storm. Reconciling the truth of what I saw with my eyes and what I heard with my ears, that was the problem.

Because it had taken so long to diagnose Payton, the cancer had a headstart. Some type of treatment had to begin immediately. They wanted to hit it hard while we searched for a doctor that specialized in this rare form of cancer. We had to at least *try* to save her life. Seven of the strongest chemotherapy treatments were thrown at the cancer. It almost killed her.

CHAPTER 10

After the diagnosis, my mind revisited trying to get pregnant for the third time.

"I hope it's a boy this time," Patrick had smiled.

"Me too," I laughed as I cuddled closer to my husband.

"I mean, I'll be happy if it's a girl, too, but it would be cool to have a son. I want someone to hang out with me. Take our bikes out. Someone to chill on the couch with me and watch TV. Yeah," he smiled hard, "That would be cool."

We had already been blessed with two beautiful daughters. First, there was my Savanna. Her name was almost Cierra but the best out of 5 flips of a coin said otherwise. We gave her two middle names; Jade because I love the stone and Sybil, after my mother.

Two years and a month after giving birth to

Savanna, Sydney Willow came into our lives. One of my favorite authors is Sydney Sheldon and Patrick always admired Willow Bay, the newscaster. There you have it. Our two girls.

Trying to keep up with Savanna, Sydney hit her milestones quickly. When she conquered potty training early, I knew she was getting out of the way for another one but I tucked that thought in the back of my mind.

With two little ones under foot, I gladly stopped working and became a SAHM (Stay-At-Home-Mom). Patrick made more than enough money to take care of us, so I was free to do what my heart loved, mother my girls.

Things were going really well. Patrick excelled as an Executive Recruiter and we moved into our dream home in Pennsylvania. Four thousand plus square feet of beautiful. Four bedrooms. Three and one-half baths. Full basement. Custom bar. Playroom. Man of my dreams. Daughters of my heart. Home right out of a magazine. Man, you couldn't tell me I didn't have it all. I simply couldn't ask for more. But I did.

CHAPTER 11

"Hi Mommy! Hi Daddy!" Payton smiled as she returned to her traumatized parents in her hospital room.

Walls up. Back straight. Bite your lip. No tears. Suck it up, Holly.

"Hi baby! Did you have fun upstairs?" *Five weeks. All you have is hope.*

"Yes! I played Bingo and I wore a cool hat! It was fun but I'm ready to go home."

Patrick caught my eye and took over.

"We can't go home just yet. We have to, uh, stay a while so we can make you feel better."

A 4-year old can't comprehend cancer so we explained it to her the best way we could with visualization.

"Payt, you have something like rocks (tumors) in

you that we need to get out. You have to have some treatments, shots, and medicine to get rid of the rocks and make you feel better. Daddy and Mommy are going to be with you all the way. Okay baby?"

"Okay," she shrugged, confident in our words to her.

Patrick and I couldn't stop hugging her. She didn't understand what we were facing or what had been said behind closed doors. An invisible clock ticked so loudly in my head, it was hard to focus. We planted our feet and prepared for the battle of our lives.

CHAPTER 12

Patrick and I barely spoke to each other for the first 3 weeks after we received Payton's diagnosis. Literally, outside of very basic answers to important questions, we did not speak to each other. I suppose as long as we did not have a real conversation, we could cushion ourselves from the overwhelming truth fighting to make its way into our world. Moreover, we didn't know how or what to say to each other. No one expects cancer to show up, especially not in a young child. We didn't know WHAT to do or how to exist.

I remember Patrick and I sitting in our bedroom, looking at each other, completely distressed, although important decisions had to be made and quickly. The first…if we were going to face this giant together or separately. We basically lived in the hospital and when we weren't there, you could find me weeping in my closet at home and him distraught with his friends.

Sitting there, facing each other, we were forced to make a decision. Drifting apart, we decided to talk. Really talk.

I truly believe that conversation saved our marriage, as we confirmed what we already knew… our personalities and our needs are different. Patrick needed to be around people to stay encouraged. I needed quietness to calm the onslaught of thoughts constantly trying to pull me down and a place to safely fall apart before emerging with my game face. We decided that he would continue to spend time with his friends and I would continue to find refuge in the four walls of my closet. We understood each other. We no longer felt abandoned by the other but rather, anchored. Appreciating and accepting the way we dealt with the crises, we joined forces as a couple, as one to fight for Payton's life.

CHAPTER 13

I don't know where my family would be without the support we received during that time. Perhaps it's possible but I don't know how anyone, unless forced to, can face a tragedy, overcome a major obstacle, or survive some of the things life dishes out without real support.

My mother quit her job in Pennsylvania, moved into her Florida "winter" home, and provided a stable schedule for Savanna and Sydney. At the time, they were in the 4th and 2nd grades, respectively. Patrick and I didn't want our family to fall apart so we gladly accepted her huge sacrifice.

"Don't worry about the girls. I'm here. I'll make sure they get to school. Homework. Activities. Dinner. Baths. Don't worry. Mimi's here."

"Thanks Syb," Patrick said, hugging her.

"Tell me this isn't real, Mom. Tell me," I said, biting my lip to stop the unstoppable tears from falling.

"It's real. This is real but you're not alone. We will fight." Having my mom by my side through this horrific journey, well, I don't have the words to tell you what it has meant to me. To all of us. My mother, an experienced oncology social worker, provided me the medical perspective I needed as well as the "mom-type" things I needed, like reminding me to try and sleep, eat, etc.

My weight dropped to a little over ninety pounds fairly quickly. How could I eat? My stomach recoiled at the thought. It's as if I lost my sense of taste. My entire being was consumed with helping Payton.

How did we get here?

CHAPTER 14

I couldn't help but think of the day I found out I was pregnant with Payton. Patrick and my brother-in-law, Rodney, were downstairs sleeping (that's a long story) and I was upstairs at 5 in the morning with a positive pregnancy test.

"Patrick!" I yelled. "Wake up! I'm pregnant!"

"That's what we wanted, right?" he asked, sitting up.

"Yes, but this was fast!" I said, voice full of emotion but excited. Patrick left for work and I couldn't believe I was going to be a mother again. A few hours from our crazy start that morning, the phone rang.

"Holly, turn on the news right now!" Patrick said out of breath. I scurried to turn on the television and tried to make sense of the newscaster stumbling over his words.

"A plane has crashed—"

"Oh my God!" I screamed, as I watched the second plane slam into the South tower.

"This looks to be an act of terrorism. It seems we are under attack," the newscaster said solemnly.

I touched my belly, terrified of the world I was bringing such an innocent life into. Never have my emotions backflipped so quickly. One moment, ecstatic. The next, devastated.

"Are you having contractions?" Patrick asked me months later in the middle of the night as he watched me awkwardly crawl back into bed.

"Yes, but I'm not having a baby today." I must have sounded like a lunatic!

"Holly."

"But its 3 weeks early, Patrick! Nope, not today," I grunted as I felt another contraction squeezing my uterus.

"Let me get the bag. C'mon Holly. Just call the doctor and hear what they have to say."

Rubbing my tight belly, my third pregnancy, I already knew what my doctor was going to say.

Reluctantly, I threw on my big old pregnancy sweat-pants and made my way to the truck.

CHAPTER 15

The baby's coming! It's coming!" I shouted as they prepped me for delivery.

"It just feels that way. You're not ready to deliver yet," a nurse volunteered without examining me.

"This is a girl," Patrick said out of nowhere in my ear. "I feel it."

We wanted a boy. The doctor said I was "carrying" like I would have a boy and although my chart leaned toward a girl, we'd planned for a boy. The room was painted blue and I'd found some cute little outfits.

"It's a girl," Patrick repeated.

"Wait, we don't have a name for a girl! Uhhhhhhhh!!!!!"

"Don't push, Holly!"

"A girl. What about Payton?" Savanna had a little friend named Payton and I'd once read about an amazing city in Hawaii called Makenna. Payton Makenna!

"I need to push!" Everyone in the room received the confirmation when my hospital gown was flung back.

"She's crowning!" a voice shouted.

"You're doing great," a nervous Patrick offered.

In the rush, my doctor entered and was not told that there was no time for the epidural. Her scalpel sliced me.

"I'm dying," I said to Patrick, shaking from the pain radiating through my body.

My little one came into the world quickly, like an avalanche rushing down a slippery slope. I should have known then that we had an unstoppable force on our hands.

"And it's a girl!" the doctor announced, plopping a big baby on my chest.

I found my footing fairly easy with three little ones. Don't get me wrong, I was completely exhausted and sleep deprived but I was happy. I would have had one more if I thought I could've given each child enough of me. Patrick and I decided 3 children were enough for us: 5 years old, 3 years old, and a newborn.

CHAPTER 16

A couple of months after her diagnosis, Payton was fast asleep as I looked out of her hospital window and watched the most beautiful fireworks dance across the sky.

I thought about everyone having an awesome time barbecuing, drinking beer, and getting bit by mosquitos. Why couldn't that be our story? Instead, my family was divided in different locations because my baby was dying from brain cancer.

The holidays should have found us together like the year before. We were…scattered. Instead, Savanna and Sydney traveled with my mom to Pittsburgh to be with family. Patrick was home trying to rest. Since we were forced to work in shifts, I called him just to connect and cried softly as not to wake up Payton.

You know the sound ice makes when you stand on it and your weight is too much for it to bear? I could feel the cracking beneath my feet.

CHAPTER 17

Our primary assignment was to find doctors that specialized in the particular cancer attacking Payton's body. We looked at the top 5 doctors and hospitals in North America.

"There's a doctor at Duke Medical Center," Patrick announced, returning to the room where my mother and I were talking one day. "He is listed as the best in the country. I can't pronounce his name. They call him Dr. G."

"We HAVE to get her there. Payton's current hospital is providing the best care they can but they don't have a Pediatric Neuro-Oncologist. Duke's Brain Tumor Center is one of the top centers and has the type of doctors we need."

We read through all of our options and chose Duke because of their experience and it was close enough for the girls to visit.

I saw a new light dawn in my husband's eyes. A light, like my own, that flickered when we were turned down for Proton Therapy by two major centers.

Unlike normal radiation, the proton therapy sends protons to the tumor only. Therefore, healthy tissue is not affected, thereby reducing side effects. However, when Payton's diagnosis became clear to those centers, we were rejected. It's as if everyone thought there was no point in trying to save her life.

"I don't know how long we will be up there, so I'll make some calls and start packing," Patrick threw behind him.

My husband. I don't mean to brag but the truth is the truth. I wish every one of you had the chance to experience him. No, he's not perfect. Who is? But he's pretty awesome!

He, alone, spoke to Payton's doctors. I couldn't. On his back, he carried the weight of devastating report after devastating report and he never complained. I will forever be grateful to him for his constant strength. It lifted me from the pits of despair.

"Girls!" I called out. All three came. I began to tell them about the possible trip to North Carolina. My mouth moved quickly over the details, trying to lighten the moment. I tried to handle the situation as best as I could but truth be told, there was *another me*. The inside angry me.

Why can't everything be okay? t*hat me* raged. *Leave my daughter alone!* She screamed to our invisible enemy, *"Leave us alone!" That me* wanted to swing my arms, break all the plates and glasses on the island. *That me* wanted to run through the living room, snatch pillows off the couch and pull DVD cases from the stand. *"AAAAAAAHHHHHH!!!!!!!!!!!!,"* t*hat me* screeched, before collapsing on the floor in tears.

"Mommy," Savanna said softly, interrupting my mental episode, "Can we go with you and daddy?"

"Not this time baby. Mimi will be here with you and Sydney. We will talk with you every night before bed, ok?"

"Okay mommy," Savanna agreed before pulling Payton back to her room.

"Sydney, we'll call you, ok?"

"Ok," she said too quiet for my heart.

"Come here and give me a hug. You know we love you. We have to take your sister to a special doctor so we can try and make her feel better."

I remember the next moment like it was yesterday. It was bedtime and Savanna and Sydney were crawling into Savanna's bed because they didn't like sleeping alone. Savanna looked directly at me and asked, "Is Payton going to die?" *How could five little words knock the wind out of you?*

"We don't know," I answered honestly. I didn't want to lie and say Payton would be better just in case things didn't work out, because my girls would lose all trust in my word.

"We're going to think positive and Daddy and I are going to do everything within our power to make your sister better. Okay?"

"Okay Mommy."

"Go to sleep," I said, smiling.

Off I ran to my closet. I barely made it inside and covered my mouth with a long-sleeved Oxford shirt before I started howling like some type of wounded animal.

All knew not to disturb me while I was in the closet. I cried until I was hoarse. Until I had nothing left. Only God knew that Patrick was on the other side of the door crying too.

"Holly, you don't know us but we read your blog and wanted you to know that you have our prayers. We live in the Philippines. God bless you!"

When Payton slept, Patrick & I would sign onto the web and read the blog posts to keep hope alive.

"We are sending you a prayer shawl," another woman wrote. "Wrap it around your daughter. We believe God will heal her. You and yours are always in our prayers."

"Be strong. I know it isn't easy to keep believing Payton will get better but have faith. All things are possible."

CHAPTER 18

"Hi, I'm Sridharan Gururangan," said a petite man with smooth bronzed skin when we arrived at Duke. "Most people call me Dr. G."

"Nice to meet you. Patrick," Patrick said, shaking his hand. I followed suit.

"Holly."

"As you may know, I am a Pediatric Neuro-Oncologist here at Duke. Here is my card with my pager and cell phone numbers. Call me if you need me, anytime."

"And who do we have here?" he asked, turning to Payton, who was eagerly waiting her turn for Dr. G's attention. "What's your name?"

"Payton," she answered proudly.

"That's a beautiful name, Payton. I'm Dr. G. I will

be your doctor while you are here and we'll try to make you feel better. Okay?"

"Okay," she said, holding up her thumb.

Dr. G held up his.

"Do you want to thumb wrestle?" she asked.

"Sure," he said.

Unbeknownst to us, while Dr. G. was thumb wrestling Payton, he was scanning every ounce of her. Her eyes. Her smell. The color of her tongue. Her posture. I mean, excellence speaks for itself. His bedside manner could be used as a how-to guide to treat parents and families. Dr. G.'s entrance into Payton's hospital room and our lives felt like rain falling after a season of drought. Refreshing. Calming. Peaceful.

"OK, you win," he announced.

"You have to give me a dollar. I always get a dollar when I win," Payton extended her hand for her reward.

"I understand," he smiled, playing along. He reached into his black slacks and pulled out a dollar bill for Payton.

"Thank you," she smiled.

"You are very welcome. Excuse me for a moment. I need to talk to your dad."

As stated previously, I didn't speak to the doctors.

My heart couldn't take it. I took my place by Payton's side while Dr. G spoke to Patrick outside the room, giving it to him straight.

"Payton does have a very rare, relentless cancer. There is no protocol to follow for this type of cancer. I will do everything in my power to help your child," he said to Patrick. "I cannot make *any* promises."

"Thank you so much," Patrick said.

As soon as most doctors heard the word Medulloepithelioma, we got "the look". The *poor parents, your daughter is about to die* look. Not with Dr. G. We finally felt heard. Seen. We felt as if we mattered.

Because Patrick is a research addict, he'd read almost everything about him before he walked into our room. Inwardly, I prayed that this doctor could do the impossible and save my daughter, that he possessed some magical knowledge to cure her. I'd heard everyone say 0% survival rate but my brain could not comprehend that number, 0. A miracle had my daughter's name on it and I truly believed in the deepest part of me that Dr. G. would lead us there.

CHAPTER 19

A few weeks after Payton's diagnosis, Jessica, my 7 year old niece, decided to cut Payton's hair, mullet-style!

"Oh my God! Jessica! What did you do?" I shouted, looking at Payton with one side of her beautiful blond hair chopped off.

"We were playing and I cut Payton's hair like they do in the movies."

You would have to see Payt's hair to appreciate how beautiful it was. Long blond curls framed the cutest face.

So many changes were going on inside my world, seeing Payton's missing hair put me into a frenzy. Patrick and I were furious when it happened but now, looking back, I think it was a way to prepare all of us for Payton losing her hair.

After Payton began chemotherapy, her hair fell off in clumps and I could tell it really bothered her. Always the little diva, she would do her hair, put on her eye shadow, and paint her nails. My mother-in-law, Linda, was a hairdresser. She came to the hospital to cut it all off so she wouldn't have the distress of losing her hair each day. It was so hard for her to do it but bravely, she cut it.

I remember looking at Payton's bald head and thinking that we would have such a story to tell after it was all over. We were all still very much in shock from the newest unwelcomed member of our family. Cancer.

CHAPTER 20

D r. G. wasted no time and was intensely focused on Payton's treatment. He did not make promises of survival, but we felt his unspoken vow to stand with us and against this horrible disease. Payton received chemotherapy for a week at Duke. We returned home, hopeful that all of our efforts were making a difference.

Dick Vitale, who is a mighty champion for families battling pediatric cancer, invited us to a fundraising event at his home. Not long after arrival, Payton began to scream in pain. Thankfully, Dr. Morelli, the doctor that initially examined Payton, was there. He examined her and called in an order for morphine. We made it through the night but by early morning, Payton continued to be in excruciating pain.

As quickly as we could, we jumped into the car to return to the ER. Due to increasing pain, she could not sit in her car seat. I had to sit in the back and strap her in across me as she straddled my lap. Angry, frustrated tears fell from my face as I held my baby girl. My pants became wet all of a sudden and I realized that Payton had urinated on our clothes. In my lap. In my arms. My daughter was becoming paralyzed.

CHAPTER 21

We arrived at the hospital and found out that Payton had lost the use of her bladder and her right leg. The physician informed us that she needed radiation immediately.

"We want a LifeFlight to Duke now!" Patrick said.

"If you want to use the flight," the doctor shared, "you have to have a nurse and Respiratory Therapist travel with you. It's a risky flight. The cost is $14,000 and we need payment upfront.

Patrick didn't hesitate. Who would? We would worry about bills and savings later. Our daughter was dying. He pulled out his credit card for payment.

"We have to warn you that Payton is extremely weak," the doctor said.

Reliving those moments now, I can't believe we didn't go insane. Every decision put her at risk. If we left, she might not make it but she needed to be under the care of her Pediatric Neuro-oncologist, Dr. G. However, we felt confident that she should be at Duke.

On our way out, we met a Muslim woman who told us to pray while we were in the sky because she believed we would be closer to God. I'd never heard that before but I was so touched by her caring and compassion that I was willing to try.

Throughout our entire journey, we met people who practiced different religions. In my desperation, I tried them all. I wanted my daughter to live.

Payton became quite distressed a few times on the flight. Those were some of the most terrifying moments, watching them trying to keep my youngest daughter alive. *Why Payton? Why?*

"Patrick," I started, reaching for his hand as the airplane landed. Four people with bright colored scrubs were standing, waiting for us to land. Payton lay before me, strapped down. Eyes closed. Buried beneath an oxygen mask. I thought the rage and fear building next to my heart would make my chest explode. Instead, my broken heart broke again. As soon as we touched down, the team moved quickly. How things could be moving so fast and slow simultaneously, I'll never know.

Patrick and I exited the airplane and moved aside so the staff could save our daughter. I don't remember how long it took them to get her inside. What I do remember is the night being so dark. Lights from nearby office buildings and a few stars in the sky watched us.

"Let's get her right into radiation."

CHAPTER 22

Hi mom. We're here. They took her in already. How are the girls?"

"They're fine. Sleeping."

She's going to die, a very small voice whispered in my ear. I froze. I believed without a shadow of a doubt we were fighting a battle that we would win and I spent very little time thinking about Payton not making it.

"Holly! Are you still there? Holly!"

"Yes, I'm here," I whispered. "I have to go mom. I love you. Tell the girls we love them in the morning."

"Of course I will. I love you, Holly. Hug Patrick for me."

Dr. G came out of the double doors Payton had disappeared behind earlier. I saw the look on his face and ran for cover.

"I'll be back Patrick."

"Ok," Patrick said, watching me skirt away. I

walked into the ladies' room. Two of the stall doors were locked so I rushed into the last stall. I flushed the toilet so no one would hear the explosion of pain escape my throat. *God, please don't let it be as bad as it feels*, I thought as I flushed the toilet again.

"The tumor is compressing her spinal cord," the doctor explained to Patrick while I was in the restroom. "She can no longer use her bladder and is paralyzed from the waist down. Hopefully, we can shrink the tumors and it will relieve the pressure on her spinal cord. We're going to do our best."

"I know you will," Patrick sniffed, biting hard on his back teeth. He wanted to thank Dr. G but the anguish of his heart choked him. A quick shake of his head was all that he could manage.

Back home, my mother pulled Savanna's blanket over her and Sydney. Those two were inseparable and usually ended up in bed together. A smile crossed her face as she looked down at her granddaughters.

Quietly she pushed a few toys aside with her foot and pulled the door almost shut. She couldn't help herself. Standing in Payton's room, looking at her empty bed, a deep sigh escaped my mother's mouth.

"God please…My grandbaby…We need a miracle…Please."

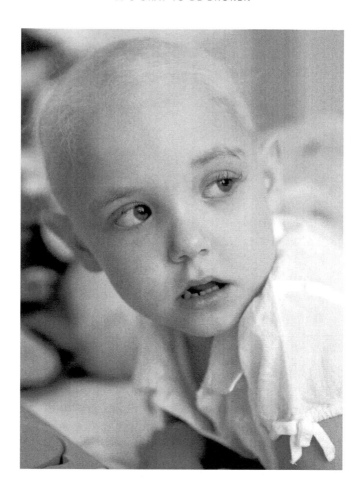

Two years earlier...

CHAPTER 23

Let's do it. Let's move. We can buy a home in Florida. Build one if we want to. Live at the beach. Bask in the sunshine. I'm tired of freezing here in PA!"

"What about work?" I asked.

"I can work from anywhere. I'll go down and set up an office."

"I can't believe we're having this conversation, Patrick. What about our home?"

"We can sell this house. Home is wherever our family is."

"This is a lot to process. I mean, it would be nice. The girls are really young so moving right now would be the ideal time to move." "Aruba ruined you," I whispered. "Let's do it! Yes! Goodbye snow! Hello sand!"

We listed our home and I began to research neighborhoods and schools. I'm not a person that makes huge, sweeping changes quickly but I had to admit, I was excited to think about our new chapter in Florida. Our house hit the market and within 2 days, Patrick pushed the sold sign into the ground. In a whirlwind, we commenced to purge and pack. Bittersweet described our last week in Pennsylvania. We were leaving the familiar, our families, and old roots to plant new ones.

In 2004, we moved into our custom-built home in Lakewood Ranch in Bradenton, FL. The girls absolutely loved the warm weather. The neighborhood was amazing. I found a great school and preschool for the girls. I then set my eyes on returning to work. After all, the girls were gone most of the day. Moreover, the job market began to spiral downward, so companies weren't hiring as quickly as they'd hired a few years earlier. New house. New bills. College tuition to save for. Retirement to plan.

I'd landed an awesomely awful job. Well, the job wasn't awful but the director I worked for was awful indeed. Out of respect and privacy, I will not go into too many details about that.

My heartbeat is to help children so I tried to find the best pediatric OT positions. Not an easy task.

The field is quite competitive so my strategy to secure a position required creativity.

The consensus was that a local company held an amazing reputation and low turnover rate. I called and asked if I could shadow one of the established OTs. Access granted!

After a couple of days, I made a bold offer, "If I work for you for free for two weeks and you're pleased with my work performance, will you hire me?"

"That sounds like a reasonable offer." Three days and a freak accident later, I was hired. Things were falling into place.

CHAPTER 24

As the days passed, things were touch and go. On a Friday, they told us Payton had 2 hours to live and we should call the family to say goodbye.

Denial is so strange. I heard what they were saying but I could not believe my daughter was dying. My heart felt fractured into a billion pieces. It was August. I was supposed to be taking my girls school shopping, not be held up in a hospital, telling my family to come and say goodbye to my 4-year old.

We wanted Savanna and Sydney, who were at our home in FL, to be able to say goodbye to their sister. A dear friend arranged a flight for them and close friends so we could all be together.

Tensions were high in Payton's hospital room as we tried to decide which steps to take next.

"You've had more time with her than you thought you would. Let her go." That's what the radiologist told us.

"Let her go?" I asked, hurt and lost. "How do you do that when she could improve and live a little longer?"

"What are the options?" Patrick asked.

I know they wanted us to end her treatment but the guilt would have haunted us, not knowing if we gave up too soon.

"We can take her into surgery and try or we can let her go."

Patrick and I were completely torn. At that moment, Dr. G. entered the room.

"You fought to get her here, let's fight to keep her here," he said. After a quick nod from both Patrick and I, he unlocked her bed and wheeled her toward surgery. We fought.

God, HOW did we get here?

CHAPTER 25

"Her vitals keep falling."

I'm not sure how I found myself in-between the doctor and Patrick. It's still a blur…the details. But I do remember certain phrases: Hours left to live, call your family, say your goodbyes. I don't know. There are still gaps and spaces, probably repressed for my own well-being.

I remember staccato moments. Holding onto Payton's bedrail because I thought I would faint. Watching the clock, hoping the jet with my mom and girls would arrive before Payton passed so they could say goodbye to their sister. I can recall looking at my baby, lying so still. The monitors beeped loudly.

Patrick stood close to me. Not sure who was holding up who at times. My soul, the deepest part of me, broke. I didn't know whether to pray or say goodbye. I couldn't do either. All I could do was think of my time with Payton.

"Mommy, is my tea ready?" Payton asked.

"Sure is," I smiled, placing a mug of chai tea in front of my daughter.

"Thanks Mommy"

"Give it a minute. It's really hot, Payt."

"Okay. I'll just put on my makeup while it cools off a little."

Payton and I began our morning ritual. First up, chai tea. Then, Payton had to put on her makeup. Bright pink eye shadow over one eyelid before painting the other blue.

"Look mommy," she said, proudly batting her eyelids.

"Beautiful baby."

"Is my tea ready now?" Payton touched her mug and pulled her hand back quickly.

"Still too hot."

"Give it a few more minutes," I repeated, as I did each morning. I sat down at our breakfast table across from my daughter, who was carefully applying her eye shadow. Precious moments. That was our time. Before doctors, nurses, hospital gowns, and needles, we talked about nothing over hot chai tea.

"Try it now," I told Payton a few moments later. She took a sip.

"God, that's good," Payton smiled as if she'd been drinking tea for 20 years.

"Finish your tea because we need to go."

"Okay. One more sip then I'll put on my lip-gloss and I'll be ready." Yeah, those moments. Those moments made me smile.

CHAPTER 26

The jet brought my mom, the girls, and a few of our dear friends quickly to our side. Whew, thank God they'd arrived. Disoriented, I stood in Payton's room, spent. I'd given all of the faith and hope in my reservoir. Hours passed and Payton remained with us.

We walked down the hallway, rounded the corner, and I saw a sea of faces I knew. My brain almost couldn't understand how the people standing 10 feet away from me were really there. When they got word that Payton was only given 2 hours to live, they flew in...for Payton. Friends that I knew lived states away were whispering in our ears.

"We're praying, Holly."

"We're here for you, Patrick, and the girls."

"Whatever you need. Whatever. Say the word."

"Your family has our support."

Patrick and I were enveloped in a sea of arms. Our family and friends. Without hesitation, they'd jumped on planes. Found babysitters. Packed overnight bags. Made hotel reservations while riding down the highway. Grabbed crackers and water for their dinner. The waiting room was completely full of people that made sure we didn't feel alone.

I will never forget it. There's no way, no way for us to thank them for that type of support. Only God can reward them for their love but they're warmth, compassion, and selflessness…they are etched in our hearts. They came to help us. Carry us. They came to tell Payton goodbye. But she lived!

CHAPTER 27

H olly, this is too much for the girls. Take them to the hotel. I know they're scared. Tired. Be with them," Patrick suggested while rubbing his red eyes.

"I want to stay, Patrick. Do you want to take the girls?" I asked.

"No, I'll stay." We had to split up. Payton needed a parent with her but so did Sydney and Savanna.

"I'll stay with you," Jack, Patrick's friend, threw in.

"Me too," Tony volunteered, patting Patrick on the back.

"If anything happens, call me Patrick."

"I will," Patrick hugged me and the girls.

Behind closed eyes, Payton stood a few feet away from three angels.

"It's almost time, Payton. It's almost time for you to come with us."

"But my family—"

"We will help them."

"Wait! How am I standing?" Payton asked, looking down at her little legs. "And look," she said excitedly, swinging her long blonde curls back and forth. "My hair! How did I get my hair back?"

"Right now, you see yourself at your happiest."

"Am I going to get rocks in my body?"

"No," the middle angel smiled. "Here, there is no sickness. There is no pain. Here, you are completely healed."

"Payton," Patrick whispered, leaning close to his daughter who'd returned from surgery.

"I have to go now."

"We will see you when its time, Payton."

CHAPTER 28

The phone rang at 6 a.m. the next morning.

"Holly, you need to come to the hospital."

I don't remember much of those moments, just feeling terrified.

"Last night was rough," Patrick said quietly as I entered into Payton's room.

"What? Why didn't you call me? What happened?"

"Well, number one, you know you don't like hearing the bad stuff. Number two, you needed to rest. You look horrible," he smiled, trying to distract me with a joke.

"Look who's talking," I said. There were no overnight chairs in ICU so my awesome husband and our two friends had to stand throughout the night. Patrick's eyes were so red, I wondered how he could even see me.

"What happened?"

"We were watching the monitor, Holly, and her heart rate would go from 40 something to 200. She would seize up and…she almost died twice. They used a huge needle to suction fluid from her brain. They finally took her to surgery, twice, because the shunt was malfunctioning. Around 3 a.m., I asked the doctor if I needed to get you back here and he stood there for a moment, watching her. Eventually he said, "No, we'll be okay.""

"Oh dear God," I whispered, rubbing Payton's arm. Hooked up to several monitors, she looked so small. I leaned over and told her how much I loved her, how so many people were there to see her and all of a sudden, she lifted her hand and held the thumbs up pose. We all cheered for her, including the nurses and staff, but we realized quickly that she wanted to thumb wrestle and that's what we did!

A few weeks later...

CHAPTER 29

Guess what Payton?"

"What?" she asked matter-of-factly.

"We don't have to stay in the hospital all day and night anymore."

"Really mom?" she perked up.

"Really. We're going to take you to a nearby hotel for a few days. The change of scenery will be nice. We'll be able to cook food and you can sleep in a regular bed. We still have to come for your radiation appointments but after that, if you're clear, we can go home".

"I'm so excited! I'm tired of being here. I'm ready to go home."

"I know baby."

"And I don't have to come back?"

"Probably not for six to eight weeks, if every-thing goes well," I said.

"I'm hungry."

"I know you are. When are you not?" I smiled.

After starting steroids to strengthen her body, Payton ate all the time. Her once smaller frame was now gone. It was strange looking at her at times. My mind painted the picture of Payton, pre-cancer. My eyes wanted to see *her*, but the reality forced me to see the new Payton. Bald. Puffy-faced. Weak-eyed. Still beautiful but…different.

Prayers rushed from my heart continually. I knew we were facing unbelievable odds but I knew we would come out on the other side of this horrible experience. I wanted the three weeks to pass quickly so we could return to our home in FL.

"Now, let me give you a heads-up, Miss Payton. When you get home in 3 weeks, you will be able to relax and play but you still have to do OT and PT exercises."

"Fine," Payton said forcefully.

"Luckily for you, you have your own occupa-tional therapist in me. Who better to care for you? So, hotel for 3 weeks. Then home with therapy to make you stronger."

"Got it. When do I eat again?"

"Soon you. I have one other surprise for you, Payton."

"What is it?" she grinned.

"You'll have to wait until Friday."

"Friday is too far away! Tell me now!"

"Nope. Trust me. You'll love it!"

"Okay, okay. Will I be able to go trick-or-treating after we get back home?"

"Yes, we'll take you. What costume do you want?"

"Tinkerbell."

"That's cool."

We settled into a 2-bedroom residential hotel not far from the hospital.

Radiation continued to slow the cancer down but it destroyed Payton's skin. Radiation burns and wounds covered her back and bottom, which were a new challenge for us. It appeared to be excruciating but Payton never complained.

Knock knock.

"Who could that be?" I asked innocently on Friday.

Payton didn't seem to care for any visitors. That

is, until I opened the door and Savanna and Sydney walked into her hotel room.

"Oh my God!"

Payton could barely be seen under her sister's arms. Mike, a great family friend, drove my mom and the girls up to Duke. We'd only seen them twice in three months. That's a long time to be away from your family. Having my family all in one room, even though it wasn't home, was still priceless.

CHAPTER 30

"Close your eyes," Patrick said as he pushed Payton's wheelchair through our front door three weeks later.

"Why?" Payton asked.

"Just do it, you!"

"Ok, they're closed."

"Keep them closed until we say open them."

All of us smiled without restraint as Patrick pushed Payton inside, then tip-toed towards her.

"Okay, open!" he said.

I will never forget how Payton cried when she saw the new addition to our family, a puppy named Buddy. The perfect welcome home gift.

Buddy was super excited to meet Payton. He ran around, slippin' and slidin', wagging his tail so hard we thought he would hurt himself. But his presence resurrected happiness in all of us.

His main goal, all day everyday, was to play. Payton's white counts where relatively low so we needed to restrict her visitors when we returned home from the hospital. Buddy made up for the lack of visitors. He played with the girls until his little tongue was hanging out of the side of his mouth. Often, you could often hear him lapping up water from his bowl.

Payton's body would have 6 weeks or so to recover from all of the radiation and chemotherapy. Her back and bottom really caught the brunt of the damage. We changed her diaper a lot. Turned her. Rotated her body so she could heal.

Just being in our home gifted us with peace. We weren't out of the woods yet and I know this sounds cliché but I'm going to say it anyway, "There's no place like home."

CHAPTER 31

S ydney," I whispered, shaking my 2nd grader awake. "Sydney," I repeated a little louder.

I hated to wake her, because it was around 3 a.m. Payton, even after her meds, cried from a bad headache and asked for Sydney.

"Yes Mommy?"

"Payton needs you baby. She has a headache."

"Ok," she said, throwing her blanket away quickly.

I watched my daughter move without hesitation to my bedroom. We could hear Payton moaning. I stepped back to see the unexplainable. Sydney gently climbed onto our bed, where Payton slept 100% of the time, and nestled close to her sister.

"Sydney."

"I'm here Payton," she assured her and placed her little hand on Payton's head.

"Your headache is gone. Your headache is gone," Sydney repeated as she touched her. "Your headache is gone." She must have repeated that sentence for over 10 minutes.

"It's gone Sydney."

"Okay."

"Thank you Sydney."

"You're welcome Payton. I love you."

"I love you too Sydney."

On more occasions than I can count, Payton called for Sydney, in the middle of the night or while Sydney was watching her favorite TV shows in the evenings. I even picked Sydney up from school on occasion because her touch could, at times, do what meds could not. Sydney always showed up for Payton. I can't explain it and I don't try to.

We were only home for a few days before we landed in our regular chairs at the hospital. Payton came down with a fever, 101.4. Fevers equaled an automatic 3-day stay, at least. I dreaded telling the girls that another hospital visit would divide our family, so Patrick told them.

"Payton has a fever so mommy has to take her back to the hospital. I will be here with you, okay?"

Savanna fell into tears. Sydney didn't say a word. Just looked at me for a moment and went into her room.

Patrick and I settled into a rhythm, balancing our schedules. He stayed with the girls at home at night and I and my overnight bag took our place at Payton's side in the hospital. Then, vice-versa.

I wrote in our blog:

There will be a day when I will write in my updates these two magical words, 'miracle' and 'cancer free'.

CHAPTER 31

"Mommy, can I get in the tub?" Payton asked. "I'll hold her," Sydney volunteered excitedly.

"Okay," I said, watching both girls smile widely.

"I'm so scared I'll hurt you, Payt," Savanna explained to her younger sister.

"No problem, 'Nana. You do other stuff for me."

"Okay you two. Let's get your night clothes ready first."

I ran a warm bath and Sydney jumped in, splashing water.

"Okay, sit all the way back Sydney," I said.

"Here we go Payton. Hold onto my arms."

I'm a little bitty thing so even though my daughter was young, a fair amount of strength was required to lift her out of her wheelchair, undress her, and lower her into the tub. Payton smiled as the water enveloped her.

"Ahhh!!!!" she relaxed against Sydney.

Two years earlier

Arrrghhh!!!!!

Patrick and I jerked around when we heard Savanna and Sydney screaming in the tub behind us.

"What is it?" I asked with my heart beating like crazy.

"What happened?" Patrick questioned.

"Payton did a stinky in the tub!" Savanna screamed, standing as far as possible from Payton.

Only then did we notice Payton laughing.

"What?"

Patrick grabbed Sydney and Savanna out of the tainted water.

"Payton, that is not funny," I said, trying not to laugh.

"Yes it is!" She laughed.

"Don't let me fall Sydney," Payton said leaning back on her sister in the tub.

"I won't let you fall. Lean on me," Sydney said then and in many different ways during the days to come.

CHAPTER 33

"Mom, can I put on my costume now?"

"We don't leave for a while, a few more hours Payt."

"I can't wait mom. Please!"

"Okay. Let's put it on you."

Her costume didn't fit. The steroids. We quickly created a costume.

"Is it time now?" Payton asked, again!

"No, when the little hand is on the six and the big hand points to the 12, it will be time to go."

"It's taking forever." Finally, it was time.

"Okay, I'm ready to stand up and walk," Payton announced at 6 o'clock.

Patrick and I looked at each other, confused.

"Remember," Payton started since we were obviously forgetting something. "You said you would take me trick-or-treating. I'm ready to walk."

That's when it hit us. She thought she would be walking as she did in years before.

"I'm sorry baby. I meant we would take you in your wheelchair."

"No!" she screamed. "I want to walk!"

Patrick tried to console her.

"No! No! I want to walk! I want to walk!"

Payton never complained and it broke my heart that I couldn't give her that one thing. I knew we had to be direct but positive. Positive but realistic. Realistic but hopeful. We tried to lift her heart. After many tears, we all set out to have a little fun for Halloween.

Payton sat in her red wagon. As we made our way around the neighborhood, her mood lifted until we ran into one of her playmates. He hadn't seen her in months and literally screamed when he did. We tried to think of the right words to repair the damage he'd caused but before we could, Payton put her head down and said, "Take me home. I'm ugly."

"No you're not!" Patrick corrected.

"Just take me home."

I admit it was a rough night. It took a lot of time with her dad and a few pieces of candy to lift her spirits.

"She's been good," Patrick said, sitting at his desk flipping through bills.

"I know. I didn't want to jinx it. She's eating. Playing. Healing."

"Yeah," he agreed, distracted.

"How bad is it?" I asked but I didn't really want to know the answer. Patrick took a deep breath.

"It is what it is. If it keeps Payton alive, it doesn't matter."

"How's work going?" I asked.

Patrick laughed. "Don't ask. Let's focus on getting through this phase. She's getting stronger Holly."

"Don't say it Patrick. I have hope but I don't want to get my hopes up. Does that sound crazy?"

"Not at all," he answered pulling me into a well needed hug.

CHAPTER 34

December 4th
From the day we scheduled this particular MRI for Payton, I became a nervous wreck. Excuse me, I misspoke. I became even more of a nervous wreck than I already was. The results would determine if all of the radiation, chemotherapy, natural meds, meditation, etc., had worked.

My chest tightened every time I thought of that date. Body started falling apart. Stomach was one big knot and always nauseous. My back, tense. My heart, broken.

On Thanksgiving, I stared at Payton so long she asked me what I was thinking about. Honestly I was thinking about the moment they told us she only had a couple of hours left to live. Yet, there we were, a family, sitting around the dinner table eating together.

A few days after Thanksgiving, we were back—you guessed it—in the hospital and a CT scan revealed that there was excess fluid on Payton's brain. Excuse me if I don't recount every specific detail. We have a blog that does. I'll just say on November 29th, Payton needed surgery right away. I hoped it wasn't a bad sign.

I stood beside her bed that evening, watching her sleep. She looked so peaceful. Her eyelashes, dramatically long and perfectly curved, rested on her cheeks.

The next day, the surgery seemed to be successful as Payton felt better and no headaches were reported. I think I took the headache from her because a migraine settled in behind my left eye.

5 more days. I thought. *December 4th...*The MRI would tell it all.

December 4, 2007

CHAPTER 35

The tumors are smaller and there are less of them" the doctor reported excitedly. I was so happy and relieved that the MRI report was in our favor, you could have knocked me over with a feather. My nose was so red from crying happy tears, I looked like Rudolph.

The weekend leading up to the MRI was beyond anything I've ever experienced. My nerves were completely shot! I couldn't sleep and I couldn't eat. I'm sure my husband was overwhelmed, dealing with my worries and his.

I did what we all do when we want something very badly...we ask God for a sign. I asked Him to let this MRI be a positive sign so I would know if Payton would live or pass. Of course, I knew we still had a long road ahead of us but I wanted reassurance that we were obviously moving in the right direction.

We sent the report to Dr. G. at Duke just to confirm. I knew I wouldn't be able to rest until I heard him say that he totally agreed that the tumors were smaller and the number of them was reducing. A day later, he confirmed the report.

On December 4th, I remember writing the word 'miracle' in our blog. Indeed it was.

A YEAR EARLIER

"Move it a little to the—"

"Hurry Holly! This Christmas tree is heavy!"

"To the left," I laughed as Patrick dropped our new Christmas tree on the floor.

"Who wants to help decorate the tree?" I asked.

"Me!" Three little voices shouted.

Christmas definitely held a new and deeper meaning for us the next year. I think there are levels of understanding and that Christmas I understood things to a greater degree. What it meant to be happy. Grateful. Content. My family circle had not been broken and I could ask for nothing more.

CHAPTER 36

One early afternoon, Payton felt really bad. That day was the only day she ever saw me cry. Somewhere between cleaning poop and vomit, I lost it.

I tried to stop myself but none of my tricks worked. I bit my lip. I pinched myself but it was too late. The floodgates opened. I wept openly in front of my daughter. I was exhausted and fed up with cancer.

"Payt," I said with tears streaming down my face, "You know I would take this from you IN A SECOND if I could, don't you?"

"Yes mommy, I know you would." We held onto to each other. I needed her just as much as she needed me.

Payton's MRI confirmed that the radiation shrunk her tumors but were still there. We wanted them gone. Once again, we would have to wait and see if they would shrink or grow. We would not have another MRI until February 7th, 2007. Another date! I didn't know how I was going to survive the next couple of months.

What we could do was create a memory. Guess who got to sit on Santa Clause's lap? Yes, she did! Those 'regular' moments really helped.

The Bradenton Herald newspaper decided to run a story on Payton. We were grateful for every opportunity to raise the awareness of childhood cancer. I realized that many people simply didn't know much about the subject. Neither did we until it touched our home.

"I am so sick of everyone talking about Payton Wright. Geez! Can you say overkill? We get it! Your daughter has cancer. She's not the first person and won't be the last. Enough already!"

"Savanna, my mommy said she's so sick and tired of hearing about your sister having cancer. We all get it!" a child said to Savanna during lunch at school.

"Mommy, stop tickling my toes!" Payton giggled as I painted her toenails.

"Wait! You can feel me touching you?"

"Yes!" she giggled as I tickled her toes again.

"Patrick! Girls!" I screamed. I'm sure I scared them to death.

"What's wrong? What's wrong?" Patrick asked.

"Payton has feeling in her toes and here on her foot again!" I cried.

We spent about 30 minutes tickling her foot. How perfect. Almost a year before she was crying in pain as the tumor was pushing its way into her spine. Now, she was crying from laughter as we tickled her.

February 7, 2007

CHAPTER 37

The cancer has spread."

BAM!!! Those words tackled every bit of wherewithal we had left.

"I, I don't understand. She's stronger. She's energetic. You saw her! She's—"

"I'm so sorry."

"But she looks healthier and...and...better," I stuttered. I couldn't manage to put the right words beside each other to make sense.

"Her body cannot be exposed to any further radiation. She's had all a human being can take."

"So what do we do? What? Where can we—?"

"This cancer is so aggressive. It will not stop until—"

"Until it kills her?" I finished.

No more running to the closet for me. No more hiding. I wept the way a mother is supposed to weep when she's finally understands her daughter is dying.

"What's wrong, Mommy? Why do you keep crying? Are my tests bad?"

"No baby," I lied (and don't you dare judge me). What did you expect me to say when my 4-year old asked how she was doing? Let's look at the alternative answer: *"Mommy's crying because you're dying."* See? I'm not saying it was the right thing to do but it's what I did to keep her momentum moving forward. Patrick and I told Savanna and Sydney what the report meant and they broke into little tiny pieces.

"Are you sure there's nothing else we can do?" we pleaded.

"I'm sure. You had your miracle already. Spend this time creating a few more memories. Let her have fun. Embrace the time you have with her. Tell her you love her. Then…then let her go."

"God, please heal me and give me strength. Thank You for sending Your angels to me."

"Payton! Are you talking to me?" I asked.

"No, Mommy. I'm praying to God."

"Oh, okay," I said, taken aback. We've always been spiritual but never overly religious. Somehow, Payton had found God on her own.

"God, I know my family will be sad if I leave them. Please help them be strong. Thank You for helping me. I love You. Payton."

CHAPTER 38

Holly, I called Tidewell Hospice—" Patrick said quietly.

"You did what?" Freaking out, I ranted until I could barely breathe.

I'll never forget the way he looked at me, like he really pitied me.

"I'm not in denial. I feel like you're giving up," I said, voice shaking.

"Holly, listen—"

"I will not give up hope," I repeated in a tone that warned him not to try me. "We have to be hopeful and speak positively."

"Be positive but hospice offers a number of services that can help us. They can come here and check Payton, do her blood work. She doesn't want to be in the hospital anymore and this will allow her to get the care she needs and let her stay home."

"Okay," I finally conceded and walked out of the bedroom.

Three angels stood before Payton. This time, my grandmother stood with them.

"It's time to start letting go Payton," the angels said.

"Okay. I love it here! I feel happy and my body doesn't hurt. But my family…"

"We will help them."

"Promise?"

"Promise."

"Especially my sisters. Savanna feels helpless and Sydney keeps it all inside.

"They love you very much Payton."

"I love them too but they don't know how to let me go."

"Then you let them go first."

"Okay."

"It's time to wake up now."

"But I don't want to wake up. I feel so good when I'm here."

"Soon…"

"Happy Birthday Payton!" we all shouted when Patrick brought her into the dining room where our family and friends had gathered to celebrate her 5th birthday.

We had a blast! I watched my daughter's face, lit by candles. The pure joy that emanated from Payton with each gift moved me. I wanted to still time, snap my finger and make that moment last forever.

Off in the corner later that evening, Payton sat with her friend, Bryan.

"Payton, at your next birthday party—"

"Bryan, I'm not going to have any more birthdays," she shared with him only.

"Look what I made mommy," Payton smiled, proudly holding up a picture of her and Patrick. "It's for Father's Day!" We loved her crayon renderings. Payton passed away before Father's Day but what a special gift she left behind.

"Payton Makenna Wright," the announcer said. I cried my eyes out as I watched my daughter graduate her Pre-K program. I completely lost all of my composure when people started standing up for my baby!

My girl. My daughter. My fighter. Despite battling cancer, surgeries, needles, chemotherapy, radiation, and paralysis, she still went to school during the week and did her homework in the hospital. My Payton, who laughed over her 25-piece puzzles and found the strength to master coloring within the lines after days of feeling weak. My example of being strong…

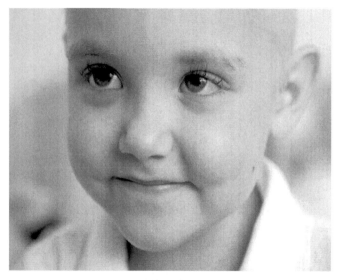

"God, please don't take my sister. I want her to live. I'm going to be angry if You let her die."

Tears rolled down Sydney's face as she lay in bed, praying.

May 17, 2007

CHAPTER 39

On May 17th, 2006, Payton was diagnosed with cancer. On May 17th 2007, an ultrasound revealed the cancer had spread in her body. Her liver and kidneys were failing.

"Mommy, my arm is hurting," Payton whispered.

As days passed, the cancer refused to stop. It wasn't enough that it had consumed most of her. It wanted all of her. It's more than anyone should have to bear, even more so a child. My family and I felt like we were spinning in the winds of a tornado. With a smile on her face, she pressed her way but her body was shutting down.

"Try and eat a few of your grapes Payton."

"Mommy, I can't see."

I looked up to see Payton's hand trying to find her bowl.

She's blind.

"Mommy?"

I could hear the fear and panic in her voice. *Think of something quick Holly.*

"Mommy!"

"Don't worry Payton," I said, as the hospice nurse administered the appropriate medication.

"It's time to sleep." I said calmly, hiding my own devastation.

"The end is near."

"How long?" we asked our doctor.

"Maybe a week."

I remember crying into Patrick's chest, torn between the guilt of wanting more time and the agony of letting my baby go.

"You better not be giving up," Savanna cried. Sydney, like me, didn't want to hear the news but we had to prepare them. Payton's health declined quickly. On Thursday, we'd scheduled a play date for Tuesday but by Saturday, it was obvious to us that Payton was nearing the end of her young life.

"Payton, why is your arm in the air?" I asked.

Payton didn't acknowledge me. I gently pushed her arm downward and she found the strength to push mine away. Again she lifted her arm as if she were reaching out for something. I could not see the three angels reaching out to her.

"Baby I know it's hard but you have to try and get up. Eat…"

"I'm not hungry," I answered. "I know but your body needs something. You haven't eaten since yesterday morning. Can I get you something?"

"No."

"I love you Holly."

"I love you Patrick."

CHAPTER 40

As much as possible, I held Payton and rocked her. It took me back to the days when she was a baby. Due to severe acid reflux, she and I spent her first eight months upright in a rocker. There I was, four short years later, rocking my beloved again.

I didn't want my baby girl to die but I couldn't allow her to keep suffering. We were informed the very end could be brutal, that she could possibly bleed out. We didn't want the girls to experience that. After all, they were just little kids. I barely knew if I could bear seeing it happen.

We arranged for a friend to take the girls out to lunch on Tuesday. While they were gone, Payton's breathing became very labored. My mother and I were in Payton's room, watching, waiting for Payton's next breath. The gaps between became longer and longer. She took a long breath and her chest did not rise again.

"Is that it, mom?" I asked but before my mother could answer, Payton took another breath.

"Go get Patrick. Quick!" my mom said.

"Come home Payton. It's time. Come with us," the angels beckoned. This time, Payton stepped toward them.

"Hi. Welcome to Friendly's," the perky waitress said. "What can I get you to drink?"

"I'll take sweet tea."

"I'll take a Sprite."

"Just a water for me."

"Okay, I'll be right back."

"You girls sit here and look over the menu. I'm going to step right over here and speak to a friend," pointing to a table across from them.

CHAPTER 41

Patrick had stepped into the other room to speak to a close friend of ours and when I came around the corner, he knew. The three of us sat down close to Payton, touching her, wanting her to know that we were with her. Payton released a long breath and the next did not come. Her lips began to turn blue.

"Come home Payton," the angels sang.

"No Payton!" Patrick shouted, surprising us. "You have to fight baby! Don't leave me!" he begged.

"I'll be right back," Payton said to the angels. She gasped and once again, was on this side of the world, with us.

Patrick and I looked at each other. More tears than can be numbered fell from our eyes, and his pleaded with mine for another option. I had none to give.

"Patrick, tell your daughter she can go." I'd never seen my husband so heartbroken. "Tell her. Tell her you'll be okay. She came back for you. She's waiting for you to tell her it's okay to go."

"Payt, we love you Payton. You did great baby. You did really good. More than good." Patrick clenched his teeth and tears filled his eyes. He could not bring himself to say the words.

"Say it Patrick!"

"You can go baby, I love you. I love you Payton. Can you hear me Payton? I love you baby. You can go now."

The three of us repeated 'I love you,' again and again, imagining her ascending to the heavens. We wanted her to be able to hear our voices all the way up.

Welcome home Payton. Here, there is no pain. Here, there is no sorrow. Payton joined hands with the angels and moved into perfect peace.

One last breath and my daughter was gone.

Sydney speaks...

CHAPTER 42

My mom's friend Nicole, who had taken us out, pulled her cell phone out of her handbag while we sat in a Friendly's eatery. As she listened to the voice on the phone, her face crumbled as she walked swiftly to us.

"Sorry girls," she said throwing a $10 bill on the table. "We have to go. Come on."

"But we haven't eaten," Savanna reminded her.

"I know. Your parents want us to come back."

We almost ran to her truck.

"Are you in your seatbelts?"

"Yes."

"Don't be scared," I said to Savanna but I could tell something was wrong. I watched Nicole wipe her eyes as she was driving.

When we pulled up to the house my parents were standing in the driveway, holding each other. We ran to them.

"I'm sorry girls but your sister passed away."

I didn't think my mother was going to say that. I thought we would have a few more days. I thought we had more time. I needed more time.

CHAPTER 43

In Payton's room, we kissed her over and over again, telling her how much we loved her.

"I love you and I will love you forever Payton," Savanna said.

"I love you Payton," Sydney said, lying close to her sister. It was such a strange space to be in because we were touching her body but I knew without a shadow of a doubt that while her body was with me, she was happy and healed in another place.

The most beautiful peace embraced me. I thought I would be angry and seething with bitterness, but knowing my daughter would no longer be tortured by this disease relieved me.

My mother and the hospice nurse bathed Payton's body. I couldn't do it. We all dressed her in her rocker clothes and painted her nails. I can't describe that whole process. It was...was...holy.

Before we knew it, Payton's friends began to arrive to say goodbye. I thought they might be afraid but her friends crawled up onto her bed and said their last words to her. Some kissed her. The sweetest words came from them. Almost 100 people passed through our home during those next hours to let Payton know how much she was loved.

CHAPTER 44

O h my God!" a neighbor cried. "Thank you so much for calling to let us know."

"What's wrong mom?" Payton's friend asked.

"Payton passed away baby and…and…mommy's sad because she's gone. She's in Heaven now."

"Will she still be sick?"

"No. She won't be sick anymore."

"Then I'm not sad. I don't want her to be sick anymore."

"That's very sweet and brave of you to say. Do you want to go over and say goodbye?"

"Yes."

"Mom?"

"Yes sweetheart"

"I think I am sad that Payton's gone." she said, grabbing her mom's waist to cry.

"It's okay to be sad."

"A Poem for My Sisters"

3
2
1 rises
1 day the
2 of you will see me again and the
3 of us will be as we are now
together

CHAPTER 45

You are not taking my granddaughter away in that truck," my father said sternly to the driver who'd come to get Payton's body in a regular looking work van.

I'm very grateful for that mistake because it gave us extra time with Payton. From 2:20 to 8:00, we celebrated the life of my little one. Then the hearse arrived. The funeral director himself showed up and apologized for sending the first van.

I opened the door and the surreality of the day set in deeper. People were standing around outside, looking toward our house. Cars were parked everywhere. The rudest little boy was circling the hearse on his bicycle. It felt like a million eyes were watching, watching us say goodbye. Watching our world disintegrate.

"I can take her body if you like," the funeral director offered.

"No," Patrick said. "I'm her dad. I'll carry her," he said quietly, as he lifted Payton from the bed.

"Support her head Patrick."

"I know how to hold a newborn baby Holly," he smiled as he held his third daughter.

"I know she's only an hour old but she's so beautiful Holly."

"Support her head Patrick," I repeated.

"You got her?" I asked Patrick as he carried Payton outside with her favorite blanket. As soon as we stepped outside, Sydney began screaming.

"Noooooooooooooooo!!!!" The most piercing, heartbreaking screeches I've ever heard echoed throughout the neighborhood.

We tried to pry Sydney off of Payton but she refused.

"You have to let her go Sydney," I cried, trying to comfort her breaking heart.

Exhausted and overwhelmed with grief, Sydney finally let go.

"We have to let her go baby. She's not sick anymore."

Patrick, Sydney, Savanna and I stood at the door of the car, staring at Payton. Lying there with her blanket and hospital puppy, she looked as if she were simply sleeping. *One last look. Okay, one last look.* I tried to drink her in. Closing that door was so difficult. Watching the car pull away with my daughter inside, I have no words.

Who am I? I wondered, looking into my bathroom mirror the next day. Every day, for almost all day for the previous year, I was Payton's caregiver. That's who I was. From morning until night, from night until morning, her needs were my priority.

Every morning started with tea together. Who was supposed to have tea with me? I didn't know what to do with myself.

"Mommy," Savanna said quietly, standing in my

bathroom doorway. No more words were needed. I wrapped my eldest up in my arms and tried to remember who I was before cancer hit our lives.

CHAPTER 46

W e'll be starting shortly," the minister offered. Our family met in a separate room before the funeral began. We waited for those attending to be seated. Over 800 people showed up to pay their respects to Payton. Patrick and I had made Payton's funeral arrangements in advance because we knew we wouldn't be able to think clearly after she died.

I can't believe this is happening, I thought. Since it didn't feel real, I was able to stand when we were called to line up. Slow motion. That's how I felt everything was moving.

Patrick and I leaned on each other and when we heard the music begin, we stepped forward just as we'd done through the hardest part of our lives, together. Our hearts filled with pride when I saw so many people there, all the hearts that had been touched by Payton's life.

We'd set up different stations in the church the day before, to show people who Payton really was. Her favorite things. It was such a beautiful service.

Some of us spoke. It was hard. Many cried. At some points, we smiled as we remembered my angel. Truly, it was a celebration of her life. As the doves were released, I imagined Payton just as free.

CHAPTER 47

It happened.

Years have passed and believe it or not, I'm still in shock. I gave birth to Payton. Bathed her. Smelled her. Laughed with her. Ate with her. Read to her. Played with her. Raised her. Prayed for her. Suffered with her. Said goodbye to her and yet – it didn't seem real, like I'm still waiting to wake up from an atrocious nightmare.

The intellectual side of me knew Payton was gone but my soul, no one notified my soul. Connected in a place beyond physicality, my soul ached for my little girl.

I'm not sure how the universe chooses people to succeed or suffer. I couldn't understand a method-ical process or grasp the philosophical equation that decided we would carry this unbelievable weight. *Why?*

Why me I asked, like millions of people who have experienced unfathomable losses. Unexpected losses.

A part of me knew that there was no way I could explain how my daughter, out of all of the other children I knew, would be overcome by one of the rarest forms of brain cancer known. But, I'm a thinker. Analytical. I search for the logic. It's my nature to try and figure things out. I cannot help myself. Therefore, questions upon questions haunted me. *Did I do something? Was it too much cough medicine? Reflux medicine? Did I…not give her enough vitamins? Too many vitamins? Not enough veggies?* What did *I* do? Someone needed to carry the blame. *What did I do to deserve such unwarranted attention? Why was my family, my daughter, chosen to carry such an unbearable burden?* Why did *it* happen to us?

Did I expect life to treat me special? Maybe. To be honest, I did. I thought if I treated people well, tried my best to be a *good person*, help those in need and take care of my family and friends, then I would be exempt from the cruelest side of life. But not so. Hiding in the normalcy of a typical life, it found me. Has *it* ever found you?

What is *it*? Something that causes pain in the deepest recesses of your gut. Have you ever experienced something that took your breath away? Your greatest fear? Your worst imagination? Something that makes you close your eyes and wish when you opened them again, all was different? Your *it* could be a divorce that split your world in two, that left your self-esteem shattered and your trust jaded. Perhaps a doctor has said there is nothing else that can be done. You don't have to tell me what your '*it*' is. I simply want you to know that if no one else understands, I understand. I understand what it's like to be trampled by inward pain.

It happens…in our blind spots, before we can see it coming. One knock at the door. One phone call. One text message. One word, Cancer, snatches the rug from under us. It happened to me at 2:20PM on May 29, 2007, when my youngest daughter released her last breath on this side of Heaven. She was 5 years old.

CHAPTER 48

The challenge of maneuvering through a traumatic event, regardless of what it may be, is that there is no static process toward healing. No sure fix. No exact science. We try to offer each other steps but if we were to be completely honest, really honest, I think we would admit that there is no step-by-step method to make it all better.

Elisabeth Kübler-Ross, a psychiatrist, proposed the idea that there are 5 stages of grief, DABDA: Denial & isolation, anger, bargaining, depression, and acceptance when dealing with one's imminent death. I understand the point she was trying to make. Do I believe that there are static phases of grief that we simply check off like a grocery list after we've experienced that phase? No, because we all process things differently. I know for myself, I entered in and out of these stages many times, in one day and in no particular order. At the writing of this book, approximately 8 years, 9 months, 456 weeks, 3198 days, 76,752 hours, 4,605,120 minutes, and 276,307,200 seconds have passed and I'm *still* angry that Payton is gone. A part of me will always be livid that I have to live this life without my youngest daughter.

I am constantly reminded that she's gone. Every birthday. Every holiday. Every time school starts and ends. Every vacation. Every dinner. Every cup of tea. Every time I see her friends. Every time I wake up. Every day. Every hour. Every second. Every breath I breathe is a reminder that she…is not with me.

Whenever I see a picture of Sydney and Savanna together, I smile at how beautiful they are and what amazing young ladies they are becoming. But there is a part of me, a piece of me, a pinch on the end of every smile that wishes there were three in that picture instead of two. Regardless of how good things are, how beautiful the day is, or how many awesome things happen, there is a sacred place in my soul that aches to hear Payton's voice shout, "Mommy!" one more time. Just. One. More. Time. That will never change.

CHAPTER 49

Years have rolled by and one might think that it should hurt less now. It doesn't. It hurts differently. I didn't always feel comfortable admitting that. In the midst of that terrible storm, I tried to be strong. Hopeful. No one, but God, saw the entire me. The completely overwhelmed me. The angry, pissed off me. No, they didn't see me crumpled up like an old and dirty mechanic's rag on the floor of my closet. Chest heaving. Wailing into my clothes. Mascara running down my cheeks as I begged for my daughter's life. Determined to keep some level of stability, I dragged myself to a hot shower each morning, although walking around looking like Pig-Pen would have been fine by me. I clenched my jaw to keep the tears at bay while I put on my makeup, as I needed to hide the evidence of many, many sleepless nights. People were surprised I looked so well considering what we were going through. What a performance…

I bargained for my daughter's life. Any good parent would gladly do the same, give their lives for their children. How many times I asked God to take me instead of Payton, I'll never know. When He took her instead of me, I was angry and numb. No one knew how destroyed I felt inside. Scanning eyes couldn't look deep enough to see my real agony. But it was there, luring me deeper into despondency. Suffocating me most of the time.

We were undeniably…lost. Patrick and I were walking zombies, trying our best to hold this slippery thing called Life together for Savanna and Sydney. Like dolls on the Walmart aisle, we wore plastic smiles at times, hoping the brightness of our need to protect them would outshine the darkness of our grief. We prayed that our desire to steady their world again would lighten the blow cancer had dealt to our family. But sometimes, despite biting my lip and pinching my leg, hot tears would roll down my face and the desire to look into her eyes or run my hand through her beautiful hair would bring me to my knees, sobbing. It happened. Has that ever happened to you? Have you or someone you know ever been broken?

Hurt. Broken. These two words are often used interchangeably but the breadth of their definitions differ greatly. Hurt comes and goes rather quickly if you allow it. Recovering from brokenness takes time. Not having a friend celebrate an accomplishment, hurts my feelings. Sitting in my daughter's funeral, listening to people speak of my daughter in the past tense, broke me.

CHAPTER 50

L et me share a little story with you that my friend, Nikki, shared with me:

Barbara, her mom, was talking with her when she remembered a boiling pot on her stove. She jumped up from her favorite chair and BAM, slammed her foot into the wall.

"Mom, are you okay?" she asked, watching her mother rub her throbbing foot and limp quickly to the kitchen.

"Yes, it just hurts."

The two looked on in unbelief.

"I don't know how I hit the wall," Barbara chuckled through the pain.

"Do you need to go to the emergency room?" Nikki asked as she watched her mother grimace.

"No, I'll take some Ibuprofen. That and a hot

shower should do the trick." But it didn't. And by early morning, the pain was so immense, Barbara was forced to crawl. Her toe was broken.

When I initially heard that story, I thought, that's me. For so long, I thought I was hurt by what we'd gone through but no...my heart was broken.

Consider broken bones or "fractures". There are several types but the one I want to talk with you about is the most common, a simple fracture, also known as a closed fracture. In this situation, a bone is broken under the skin. The break is not easily seen but obvious when touched. If you gain nothing else from this book, I hope you are able to capture this: Many people are living fractured. Broken. They look quite normal on the outside. They go to work. Laugh at lunch. Smile until you touch their broken place.

People who meet me for the first time now see a family of four. They see my two beautiful daughters and they are confused when I say that Sydney is my middle child...but to me, she will always be my middle child. She didn't become the baby of the family because Payton passed. Even as a young child, she would correct you herself. So whenever people asked about my third daughter, they touched my broken place.

CHAPTER 51

After a bone is broken, it is covered and protected so it can heal. Likewise, we must cover people in their grief, or when their hearts are devastated, and give them time to heal.

The age we now live in is quick. With the press of a button, we can Skype someone on another continent. Conference calls can bring groups of people together in one moment. We are accustomed to immediacy. Fixing things speedily. Fast resolutions. Instantaneous communication. None of those things apply to someone who is grieving or broken.

I wrote this book because our society is uncomfortable with broken people. We don't know what to do with brokenness. How to solve it. You can't throw money at it and make it alright. You can't whisk it away on a luxurious trip and make it disappear. Hurt may respond to those things but not brokenness.

A few months after Payton passed, I noticed that some people seemed upset with me for grieving. I felt as if I were living in a court room before a jury. Whenever I mentioned Payton, audibly or indirectly, there were *some* people who found me guilty of grieving too long. Initially, their displeasure with my pain was expressed by changing the subject quickly or becoming visibly tense. Their disdain and intolerance for my heartache then forced me to pretend to be more okay than I was.

As long as I *looked like* the old Holly and smiled like the old Holly, they were happy. But the real Holly…the one that couldn't get out of bed some days, the one who curled up into the fetal position and wept or that didn't know how she could make it from the bed to the bathroom to brush her teeth, they despised. So I wore a mask because I didn't want to lose my relationships. I needed my friends more than any other time in my life. I'd already lost more than enough for a lifetime. Desperate not to lose anyone else in my life, I tried to be the person *they* needed me to be. Happy on the outside, but the word miserable can't even describe how I felt on the inside.

Each day, I felt the pressure from my jurors. They watched me closely. Listened intently. When

I could no longer keep up the façade, the real me, the weak me, began to peek through. I didn't have strength to play the game anymore. My inner reservoir was depleted.

The evidence was on the table and after deliberating behind closed doors and in secret conversations, some of the people closest to my heart judged me guilty. Guilty of not getting over my pain quick enough. Guilty of not being the old me, I guess, and when I needed support the most, they sentenced me to living without them. In my darkest hour, some of the people I cherished the most, deserted me.

Lucky for me, a judge has the authority to over-turn a verdict if s/he feels there is insufficient evidence and eventually, I was acquitted of being a bad person for grieving for my daughter. I couldn't help but to wonder how it had reached that point, though. Shouldn't I have been released on my own recognizance from the beginning? Didn't I have a history with these people? They knew me. I shouldn't have been punished for not knowing how to handle events beyond my control.

Though some decided to leave my life, many stayed and comforted me. Much of my family and many of my friends were just…present. They didn't have a lot to say and they didn't expect me to say a bunch. They understood that there was nothing to be said. A hug or a rub on my back meant a lot. A card or an invitation to lunch, even if I couldn't go, touched my heart.

I share that with you to say that not everyone will understand your brokenness. Those who've never been branded by the hot iron of grief or been completely devastated can't possibly grasp how deeply it hurts, how strongly you feel, how overwhelming it is. Maybe the words won't be spoken but by some, an ultimatum will be issued: Be the way I want you to be now or else.

CHAPTER 52

I'm telling you this so you can be prepared. I lived through this and to some degree, still do. There are people who will leave you because they can't fix you. Think about that for a second. It's not that their hateful, they're uncomfortable. Not willing to put your need to be supported before their need to be recognized, they will distance themselves.

We like to solve problems, resolve issues, and some people simply can't handle the new you. Yes, I know you may feel old and worn from what you've gone through but still, after a painful event, you're a new you. You are indelibly changed.

There is a sacred space within my soul that only seeing Payton's face again can fill and that has to be accepted, understood. Perhaps if we can understand our limitations, we won't punish people when they don't respond the way "they should." If you can accept that there is only so much you can do, give or be to a person, you won't feel forced to try and achieve something that is unachievable. Only time can heal some wounds and even time must bow to the fact that only eternity can reconcile some things.

Patience. This is by far the greatest gift that can be given. Accept the fact that there is nothing you can say that is going to make a broken heart instantly heal. Embrace the fact that there is nothing you can do to make a grieving soul no longer grieve. Patiently, be present.

You don't have to say anything. Many times, it's better if you don't. Your efforts to comfort may be misconstrued or offensive. That "they're in a better place" may be the last thing someone wants to hear or "you can have more kids" may make someone feel you think the person they lost is replaceable. Don't be creative. Just be.

And on the other side of that, to those that are broken, know that people are trying. They want to comfort you. They want to help. They want to fix things and they feel helpless. Know that their heart wants to be there for you. Understand that it's not easy to watch someone you love, hurt.

When we can acknowledge these things in each

other, we can move forward with a mutual understanding that grief is ongoing. Some broken bones heal but they're never the same. Losing someone you love forces you to find a new reality.

CHAPTER 53

Living after a loss is a moment by moment, day by day, month by month, year by year, journey. While we were fighting for Payton's life, all of our focus and attention was on her and making sure our girls were okay. Patrick and I struggled with the basics, such as sleeping and eating. We were exhausted but couldn't sleep. At home our thoughts were full of "what ifs." In the hospital, there were all types of alarms and beeps and nurses in and out that prevented us from sleeping. I really don't know how we survived. We weren't sleeping. We weren't eating, not because people didn't offer us food in the hospital, but we just couldn't. Stress consumed us. We were consumed and haunted by the word, terminal.

Seconds after Payton passed, a huge wave of peace showered me. I can't really explain it. The carefulness with which we let her go, I felt as if God had received her and that brought me peace. But weeks after…I was numb. Lost. I didn't know what to do. I had been her caregiver for so long, I didn't know my role anymore.

Inside, I felt myself falling deeper and deeper into despair. I remember falling so low, the lowest I'd ever been in my entire life. Although a ton of support was offered to us, I felt alone. Broken. My baby girl was gone. We were in financial ruins. Deserted by some. Tolerated by others. It all came crashing down on my heart. After being brave for so long, the levee broke. The dam collapsed and inside I lost the little grip I had left.

While we were fighting for Payton's life, every doctor I met prescribed me something. Antidepressants. Anti-anxiety. Sleeping pills. They were all trying to help me make it through a horrible situation. I imagined they feared for my own life. Losing weight by the day. Not sleeping.

Hopelessness jumped on my back and wrestled me to the ground and I remember going into the bathroom and locking the door. I was tired. Tired in a way I can't really explain. I wanted to stop hurting.

I needed peace so I lined up every prescription given to me. There were 20 bottles looking back at me.

I cried as I reached for the first one. But something, probably Payton, slapped me upside my head with a moment of clarity. *What are you doing?* I sobbed uncontrollably as I thought of Savanna and Sydney. My girls had been through enough. *Imagine if you leave them.* I stood there, tired of living and tired of dying inside. Memories and unrealized hopes crashed into each other. I opened the first bottle and dumped the pills into the toilet. I wanted to live.

CHAPTER 54

That moment led to this one. I shared my story to let you know that I have been where you are and after years have passed, ups and downs, highs and lows, I want you to know that it's okay to be broken. This book is not saying you should be depressed or *live* broken. Far from it.

What I'm trying to do is address two groups: Those that are broken and those that must comfort them. If we can understand each other, we can grow.

Maybe you're reading and you've never lost anyone close to your heart or been through anything that almost destroyed you from the inside-out. Unless you're special, you will one day and you will need someone to be there for you.

Give others what they need. Your support. Space. Time. Love.

CHAPTER 55

A week after Payton passed, our phone wouldn't stop ringing, which on one hand was a good thing. People cared. On the other hand, the four of us were deep in the pit of despair. Sinking in the quicksand of grief.

I still thought I might see her at any moment. Some part of me hoped, and this will sound absolutely crazy I know, but some part of me hoped that none of it is was real.

We saw Payton in everything we did. Everywhere we turned. She was gone and a little piece of me was still begging for time with her. Despite my attempts to gather myself, the slightest wind could shift my footing.

The girls were curled up in our bed one morning, missing their sister and talking about Payton, and

Patrick announced that we simply needed to get away. Away from the phone. Away from the neighbors. Away from the people, who with good intentions, stopped by unannounced. We needed to breathe away from everyone and everything, where no one knew us, where I wouldn't have to repeat our story or explain what happened when I ran into someone who said, "But I thought you had three girls."

A cruise was gifted to us, just in the nick of time, which some people were jealous over – as if we wouldn't trade the world to have our daughter again, but that is another story. We needed to get away. Off land. The girls started to pack and I cried angry tears just thinking of leaving Payton behind.

"Mommy," Sydney said, coming to stand close to me. "Am I going to get cancer too?"

I hugged my daughter to comfort her but inside I was burning up with anger. How dare this disease take my baby and then intimidate my other daughter! How dare it loom in her mind and make her afraid? Moreover, there I stood, unable to tell her, "No."

"Let's go pack baby," I said with a smile but in my head, with every bit of strength in my soul I screamed, "FUCK YOU CANCER!"

CHAPTER 56

I could talk to you about many things. For instance, we could discuss how little funding is given to pediatric cancer research. Yes, we are saving ourselves before our children but that is not the goal of this book. I want you to know, for sure, that it's okay to be broken. I'd also like to share a few lessons Payton's life and death taught us:

GUILTY NO MORE

At times, I still question the things we put her through in order to try and save her life. We had to at least try. I wanted Payton to know that Patrick and I would do absolutely anything for her. We turned over every rock. We tried every option and the last desired option was to let her go. She was no longer truly living. The remnant of her true essence was gone. I wanted her to be healed even if that meant being with God.

Release yourself from guilt. Maybe you did everything you could. Even if, in hindsight, you see you could have done more, free yourself. You cannot truly live while carrying the weight of yesterday. You can't. Resolve the issue in your mind so you don't find yourself stuck in the same mental rut years from today. Once and for all, free yourself.

FEELINGS ARE OKAY

Patrick and the girls, we were still a family, but we were missing one. And the hurt comes unexpectedly. It reminds me of phantom pains. Have you heard of those? Have you heard of people that have lost limbs due to amputation or physical deformities and their limb is gone but you'll see their faces cringing in pain? You may even see them cry from the pain of missing something that's gone. Yeah, phantom pains. That's a great way to describe how I feel at times. I hurt in a place that I can't really touch and I don't feel guilty for it anymore. Neither should you.

MONEY MATTERS

I remember the first time I spoke with Nikki about the Payton Wright Foundation. As I shared with her the financial devastation that usually follows a diagnosis like Payton's, as well as many other cancers and diseases, she could barely speak. She didn't know. Most people don't. That's not something you talk about when you're trying to keep your loved one alive. When you leave the hospital after another devastating day, you usually don't sit down and go through your bills on the counter. You already know.

Luckily for us, we'd saved a considerable amount of money before we hit the storm. But in no time, we burned through our savings, 401(k) plans, and most of our life insurance, with no real means of bringing in enough money to match our needs. It's so strange. At one point in our lives, while living in Pennsylvania, we lived in a 4,000 square-foot home with a nice nest egg. Patrick was doing very well and

I enjoyed doing what I loved, mothering my three girls. A few years later, we were filing for bankruptcy. We lost our car. Most people did not realize how much we lost. Not even us. And we would do it all again to try and save Payton.

I share this not to sound pitiful but to expose the true financial challenges people go through while battling this disease. Imagine not having extra money. We receive news all the time about families not having power in their home or being evicted because they can't pay their bills.

It's great to support cancer research because we need a cure for its many forms but families need practical help to live every day. They need to know that during the most challenging time in their lives, they won't be evicted. That's why we started the Payton Wright Foundation, to help. Money matters.

LETTING GO

Letting go isn't easy. We tried everything within our power. The doctor said Payton had had the largest amount of radiation possible. The cancer laughed at the chemo treatments. We spent thousands of dollars on alternative medicines and natural remedies. Enough was enough. We fought. We prayed every prayer. It was time to let go. It was no longer about what was best for us, but what was best for Payton.

A couple of days before she passed, she began to reach up toward the ceiling, reaching for something I could not see. She knew she was going. Sydney and I usually handled her immediate needs. Savanna, being the little mother that she was, looked out for me, Sydney, and Patrick. But at the end, Payton began to push Sydney and me away. She wanted my mother or Savanna to help her, to change her, to talk to her. I didn't understand it then but now I do. That was her way of preparing me, for preparing us. She was letting us go. Don't be surprised if the person you are caring for lets you go, too.

PRIORITIES

Patrick and I wanted our girls to be okay. We wanted to make sure that they processed their pain properly and didn't become angry and bitter with everyone because they lost their sister. My priorities were to have them well-adjusted, as much as possible.

We were away for almost a year, as far as our attention goes. We were away from them for months on end. When we saw them each time, they were different, they had grown, physically and emotionally. At the end of Payton's journey, we needed to learn each other again. That was my priority, and making sure that Patrick and I were not closing each other out. My priorities were simple, to love my husband and my children. To find my way with them. My sanity was a priority. Getting out of bed was a priority. Taking a bath was a priority. Those things didn't come easily. It took a lot of effort. Yes, effort to stand upright. To steady myself again.

Just like a baby learns to crawl first, I had to learn life all over again. I needed to go back to work because when it was all said and done, we'd lost almost everything financially. I needed to work but I didn't have the strength to work. Do you understand this catch-22? Do you see how different our priorities were after she passed? Take care of YOUR priorities and the people that love you will understand.

SUPPORT: A NOUN AND A VERB

We noticed a lot of women, alone, while we were in the hospitals. For some reason or the other, husbands and boyfriends were absent and it made me extra grateful for Patrick. He worked. He researched treatment options for Payton. He spoke to the doctors. He stayed awake. He tried to be there for me. He paid attention to our girls. He ended up almost leading a support group at Duke because all of the other men had deserted their wives, partners, or girlfriends. I'm not bragging. I'm sharing this so that other men will be inspired to be present. To support. You are needed! And the other way around too!

Your support system is crucial when you're facing a mountain. Who you surround yourself with and allow in your world is vital. Their energy and words will pick you up or help you fall. If words are that powerful, imagine how powerful your presence or absence can be. Support!

A CAREGIVER'S GIFT

We were facing a tremendous challenge but we wanted to keep as much normality as possible. Payton had her own routine. Every morning at 6:30 or so, she would wake up and ask, "What can I have to eat?" Every morning, we would then start the day with our chai tea.

She'd put on her little makeup while her tea was cooling off. She would reach into her little red purse and get her pink and blue eyeshadow. She also had a baby's brush to brush her hair. She felt independent. We didn't try to micromanage her every move because that would've made her feel helpless. My 4-year old was facing what most of us will not have to face.

By allowing her to have some role in her requests, put her in control. That means a great deal to someone who is facing an uncontrollable circumstance. I tried to empower her as much as possible. That small gift of independence allowed her to maintain her dignity.

DIFFERENCES

Patrick and I have different personalities. We're different. Remember I shared that Patrick wanted and needed to be around people to keep him uplifted; I needed to be alone or with him. I needed quietness to focus my thoughts. After acknowledging the needs of the other, as well as the differences in each other, we were able to have a stronger connection. Nothing changed. He still spent time with family and friends and I stayed close to home, but we always felt that the other was near and available. It's okay to be different.

You may need to talk a lot to stay out of depression. Another person may want to be alone. Neither way is right or wrong. Find your way through life as you need to. Don't compare yourself to anyone else.

Losing a parent is different from losing a child. Finding out someone died unexpectedly is very different from watching someone suffer. My point is, don't compare. Every person and situation is different. Don't be disappointed or angry that someone reacts differently than you.

TALKING WITH KIDS

It's crucial to communicate with children because in our silence, they somehow attribute blame to themselves. Patrick and I worked together to make sure Savanna and Sydney knew what was going on, as much as they were able to comprehend. Sometimes they would ask, "Is Payton going to die?" I didn't want to say, "Yes."

I didn't want to say yes because I didn't know for sure if she would. Initially, she'd been given five weeks... and there we were, months later, still together. I didn't want to say yes because I wanted to leave room for a miracle, leave room for her to be the first to survive. You probably think that sounds crazy now but then, watching her defy the odds, it seemed possible. I didn't want to curse her with an absolute, "Yes." So we said, "It's possible." We kept them focused.

Whenever we received news, we tried to process it as quickly as possible so we could share the plan with the girls. We felt it was our job as parents to stand in front of them and take the brunt of the weight of what was going on. We didn't collapse and fall to pieces in their presence. We tried to be positive because we knew they were feeding off of our energy. Kids need to grieve too.

UNIQUE LOSSES

Patrick was an amazing father to Savanna and Sydney, but there was something different between him and Payton. That was his little buddy. I would bathe the other two girls while he would take care of Payton. When the other two girls were in school, he would take Payton to her daycare, have lunch with her, bike with her, and build amazing structures with

Legos. Many nights, the two of them sat beside each other watching, "Who Wants To Be A Rockstar?" Sure, she should've been in bed but I'm so glad she and Patrick had that time together.

We all lost something different. Patrick and I lost a daughter. The girls lost a sister. Four people lost a granddaughter. Her playmates lost a friend. Losses are unique.

TRUTH

The only way for someone to know the absolute truth about where you are is for you to be honest. Therefore, I suppose I should ask you at this point, Are you hurt or are you broken?

Ah, you're hesitating and I understand your hesitation. It's okay to say you're broken. I know you've probably been told to "be strong" and "move on" but you can do neither of those things until you first allow yourself to experience your truest emotions.

Let me be the voice that gives you permission to be honest. I invite you to remove the mask that others have inadvertently asked you to wear. They do this by asking, "How long has it been?" and "Don't you think it's time to…" questions, forcing you to box up your pain because *they* are uncomfortable.

Listen to me. It's okay to feel *what* you feel, *the way* you feel it. Cry. Moan. Scream. Be silent. Sing. Feel. Spend time with your friends. Be alone. I'm not giving a license for depression or the maltreatment of those around you. That's not what I'm saying at all. What I am saying is…do what you need to do to process what has happened in your life.

IT'S ALWAYS TIME FOR TEA

It takes time to make tea. The water must boil and then the tea bag must relax therein. Slow down. Take time out for the people you love. We are moving at break-neck speed from the time we wake up until the wee hours of the morning.

When was the last time you stopped and looked deep into the eyes of your child? Your friend? The person you say you love. What was the last meaningful conversation you shared with someone or have text messages replaced your voice?

Slow down.

LIFE IS MUCH MORE FUN WHEN YOU LIVE OUT LOUD

Payton was a fireball. Forget Disney songs. She loved rock n' roll! I once tried to get her to wear a nice girly dress for Easter and she would not have it! In the blink of an eye, you could turn around and see her totally naked, dancing on the coffee table! Bold and determined, Payton made no apologies for what she loved. Live out loud. Who are you? What do YOU like? What makes YOU happy? Stop living to please other people. People change. Stop pretending. Be your authentic you.

EVERY PRINCESS NEEDS A FROG OR TWO

Payton was addicted to frogs. They represented strength to her. She carried a silver one in her pocket always and wouldn't wear bottoms without pockets. She needed her frog and two little rocks with the words 'miracles' and 'blessings' inside.

The night of her memorial, the streets were

covered with frogs beyond number. I'd never seen anything like that in my life. I'd asked Payton to send me a sign that she was okay and there were so many frogs on the road, some people had to park their cars and walk. Everyone needs a frog or a reminder to fight. What is your reminder? You need one. You can't allow your grief to sit and never turn it into something meaningful.

We used our grief to start the Payton Wright Foundation to help other families who are battling childhood brain cancer. When you use what you've been through to help other people, you will find your brokenness changes into something meaningful. You need a frog. Join a fight.

HONESTY IS THE BEST POLICY

Communicate. Tell the truth about how you feel and what you need. When you're going through a difficult time, tell people if you need their presence. Or, let them know that you need some alone time to process what you're going through. Don't wear masks or pretend you're something you're not. Be honest.

Conversely, if you are trying to support someone and find yourself feeling upset that you can't help them, talk about it because if you don't, you may lose a relationship simply because you don't understand or because you feel helpless to help.

CALLING SOMEONE STUPIDHEAD SOUNDS MUCH NICER IF YOU'RE SMILING WHEN YOU SAY IT

Okay, I know how that must sound but let me explain. Children can't articulate how they feel or what they are thinking as well as adults. That's why you may see a toddler fall into a tantrum when they think you've poured more juice in someone else's cup. What they are really trying to say is…it looks like you value the other person more than me. They can't express that with words. They may just cry and flail their arms.

Sometimes, when it was time for Payton to take her medicine or get shots, she would say, "Okay stupidhead," but she would say it with a smile. Payt wasn't trying to be disrespectful. She was 4 years old having surgeries. Getting pricked and prodded.

Taking handfuls of pills. She knew she had to do it so her way to show her displeasure with the situation was to use the word, Stupidhead.

If you're a caregiver, I'm sure you understand this part. It's not easy taking care of someone that can't take care of themselves. I imagine you are often shouted at, a victim of bullying, complaints, and ungratefulness. I'm not making an excuse for that behavior but what I am doing is inviting you to see life from their perspective. It can't be easy to lose your independence. Imagine how you would feel if all of a sudden, someone had to bathe you, change your diaper. Maybe, just maybe, their anger is really shame. Perhaps, their outbursts toward you really mean, "I'm scared" or "I don't want to die." Don't get entangled in the actions or words, search for the meaning.

BE THANKFUL FOR EVERY MINUTE YOU HAVE

Time is a gift. We take it for granted but time is a true gift. Losing Payton at the age of 5 taught me a lesson I thought I knew but so often I forgot. Every breath we have should be one of gratefulness. One of the things that makes my heart okay is knowing that I was a very present mother to Payton, even before the cancer.

Life is busy. Tasks and to-do lists are ever growing but it behooves us all to stop and be more thankful. Death is a cruel teacher but I must admit that its' lessons are not easily forgotten. I try not to complain about things that don't really matter, but rather be fully present and grateful for the moments I do have. Are you really aware of the moments you've been granted? Be thankful that you're here and have a life to live.

ALWAYS, ALWAYS, ALWAYS KEEP THE FAITH

To me, religion or the things you do to express your faith are very different from your personal connection with God. Regardless of how you practice your faith, the main point is to keep it.

You must protect that which you believe when the tsunami waves of grief or depression crush your spirit. Hope. You must protect it from the vultures looming, for AS SOON AS we feel hopeless, living becomes difficult.

Keep the faith. Don't give it to cancer. To grief. To depression. No, you keep your faith. Tuck it close to your bosom. Guard it. Don't allow the happenings of life to snatch your faith!

ONE SMALL LIFE CAN MAKE HUGE RIPPLES

Payton's journey was followed by people all over the world. She's gone but her life is still touching people and will continue to do so. Her legacy will sing through the Payton Wright Foundation and through this book. So, remember what I've shared. Read this book again and again until you really know that it's okay to feel what you feel.

Lastly, I would like to end this book by introducing you to my daughter, Payton Makenna Wright. Bright. Beautiful. Energetic. Fiery. Determined. She lived her life as a giver, making sure her friends were happy and cared for.

Payton was only with us for 5 very short years but she fought a very rare cancer with a grace I've never seen before. Her stance in the face of unbelievable challenges inspires me to move forward and fight for others. Rarely did she complain and in her honor, I will live my life to help families battling pediatric brain cancer. In her honor, I pledge to support people, asking for nothing in return.

Payton, I'm so proud God chose me to be your mom. I love you more than words could express. I see you in my dreams. I feel you with me always. Yes, I look forward to the day we are together again. I didn't have you for many days but you changed my life, and the lives of many, forever. Loving and caring for you was my honor. I'm so glad I met you and the pleasure was all mine. Payton Makenna Wright, born May 7th, 2002, lives on in you and me.

PAYTON MAKENNA WRIGHT

Thank you so much for your support. I encourage you to share this book with your family, friends, and community. Please leave your thoughts and your experience with this story at www.amazon.com.

I'd love to hear from you.

I also invite you to read a detailed log of Payton's journey at www.paytonwright.org.

Holly Wright wears many hats, and two of her more prominent and passionate roles involve her work as a Pediatric Occupational Therapist, as well as, her service as Vice-President, co-founder, and public spokesperson for the Payton Wright Foundation. She and her husband started the foundation in 2008 after losing their five year old daughter, Payton, to Medulloepithelioma, a rare form of brain cancer.

The foundation provides financial support to families who are caring for a child with brain cancer by directly paying their everyday expenses such as mortgage payments, utilities, etc., when they are unable to do so. Physicians and social workers can also refer families to the foundation who are in need of resources. To date, the Payton Wright Foundation has provided financial assistance to thousands of families throughout the United States since the Foundation's inception.

Holly obtained her Bachelor of Science in Health Science and Masters of Science in Occupational Therapy from Duquesne University in Pittsburgh, Pennsylvania and currently resides in Bradenton, FL.

During her spare time, she likes to run, bake, and spend time with her family.